Blur

AUTHOR—ANONYMOUS FOR
HIS OWN PROTECTION

ISBN: 0615629954
ISBN 13: 9780615629957

Content

Acknowledgments

I want to dedicate this book to my beautiful wife and best friend for always being there for me in both good times and bad and for always providing me with positive direction. I would also like to thank my wonderful daughter for always having a healthy amount of humor and making me laugh at life. Without their inspiration and humbleness, I could never have completed this work.

Lastly, I wish to thank my brother, sister, mother, father, and friends for a lifetime of fun and excitement. They have filled my life with these wonderful experiences. Everyone who has known me through the years knows the true details behind this story, and although some events were serious, life is too short not to find the humor behind the stories.

CHAPTER 1

The Shadows

I could hear our feet splashing hard through the puddles on the downtown streets, and I knew no matter how fast we ran or how well we hid, they would not stop chasing us. Our hearts pounded frantically and uncontrollably. The blood rushed through our bodies so forcefully that we worried that at any moment, it would burst out of its vessels and kill us. Sweat dripped down and smeared our faces like a warm, sultry rain, but this was not a nice, comfortable shower. The hard pounding rain is usually an enemy to those individuals who find themselves in a situation like our current one. We should feel trapped, unprepared, unprotected, and within reach of our stalkers. After being relentlessly pursued many times in recent years, I knew the odds and was comfortable knowing that our escape was imminent, but my wife was not used to this type of activity. I felt bad about her fear and discomfort and knew I couldn't toy with our followers on this rainy evening. I had to be diligent in effecting our escape. At this moment, the rain was the only true protection we had left between us and what we knew to be a real threat from an unknown enemy who trailed our every step.

As we rounded a corner en route to our eventual exit from the fear and threat of capture by the nameless assailant pursuers lurking behind us, we could hear squealing from car tires in the near proximity and the spattering of their pursuing footsteps. We recognized their forward progress and realized they were only steps behind us. We could clearly identify the sounds of the puddles they were going through. They were splashing through the puddles we had just been through only seconds earlier. We knew our potential captors were closing in on us and we had to keep moving forward, vigilantly paying close attention to what was in front of us while not slowing down to the dangers that lurked behind us. Our fears were real, and even though we had no idea what our pursuers really wanted with us, this threat seemed genuine, as they were not giving up on the chase. Instead of stopping to answer their questions, we just kept running as far and long as necessary to get away from them. We had no plan, were not sure of our way out of this situation, and had no answers, so we just continued to run as hard and as fast as we could to stay one step ahead of them, whoever "they" were this time.

Since darkness and the glare of an occasional street light was the only thing anyone with normal vision could see on this rainy evening, I had a clear advantage as long as I could use all of my unusual senses.

Let's step back in time for a minute so I can give you a better understanding of the situation. You see, the story starts with my vision, or I should say, my *odd* vision. I was born, like everyone else, with the ability to see energy levels, or as many people call them, *auras*. Yes, I said everyone is born with the ability to see these energy levels. It's a normal sense similar to taste, hearing, feeling, smelling, etc. The uniqueness of my situation is that it is usually temporary and only available to newborn babies. It falls away from most as their other senses develop and increase in prominence and the need to see these auras disappears. For me, this added sense never went away, and this is where my story begins.

Word of my visual abilities spread as I grew older, both from people who had directly witnessed the advantages my vision had offered me in life and from many years of testing and studies performed by hospitals and scientific centers. Over time, the information leaked out and eventually made its way to the national and international intelligence community. People who manage these intelligence organizations like such oddities and request your services when they think you can help their causes, but as I learned, they do not like to be told that you are not interested. As a result, I had to avoid many direct and indirect threats from both national and international foes who seemed to take the position that if I wasn't going to work for them, then I had to be contained and prevented from working with others, even though I had no intentions of working for any of them. I always knew I was safe from any real harm, because, as I found out through the many scientific studies I had been through, only a small handful of people in the world had my condition. This gave me comfort; because of this limited population, I probably would never be killed, as that would end the hope of my ever being able to join up with any of the organizations; however, it also meant that I would spend part of my life avoiding a constant threat of being pursued or, worse, my family would be forced into uncomfortable situations, such as was the case on this rainy evening.

I knew from experience that the men chasing us really had no way of catching us, as they were running blindly in the rain and I, because of my sight differences and the effects of the rain, could actually see their every movement better than if this had been a clear evening. My visual abilities enabled us to navigate though this wet, dark evening while keeping our pursuers completely in my sights and us out of their grasp. Since I am able to see the energy levels on all living things, any movements stand out very clearly at night. When I see people moving in the dark, it's like they are running with spotlights on them. When it rains, these energy levels become blurred and much larger than they would be on a dry evening, similar to lights reflecting off of a wet windshield during an evening rainstorm.

Although these men were coming from so many different directions, the city streets, the rainy evening, the darkness, and the shadowy, tucked-away spaces all played themselves as conspirators to our ultimate escape. When I'm alone, I never worry too much about these situations, and they have presented themselves to me many times in the past. In fact, I usually enjoy them, as they remind me of a game of cat and mouse or chess. In these situations, I usually purposely play with my pursuers in a way that compounds the reality that they cannot catch me. I'll let them get close throughout the chase, giving them the feeling that they are finally about to catch me, and then I'll surprise and embarrass them with an escape that is so simple that they realize they have merely been played with, leaving them feeling foolish and used. My usual solution to pursuers is to allow them to trail me to the point where they give up for the day, and then I go to work and start pursuing them. I have often followed these people back to their homes and offices and left notes to them on their desks or beds thanking them for their part in our game of chase. My notes also often de-scribe to them how much I enjoyed watching their family members during their daily events and goings-on. I include their names and often introduce myself directly to their family members as an old friend of the pursuer. I ask them to tell them that I said, "Hello." They go home and innocently tell them what I have said. Since my pursuers generally operate in clandestine conditions, this obviously unnerves them quite a bit. When this happens over and over, the pursuers tend to go away in fear.

I'm relentless in this game of chase, because my experience has always proven to me that the best defense is a strong offense. When creating my offensive stances, I take nothing for granted, and I approach my pursuers' most-loved things, the people they love, as bargaining tools. Everyone has something they love more than their need to bother me, and they will step down from pursuing me as long as the threat of losing what they love is strong enough. Not everyone is married or has kids or families, so outward threats on others around them don't always work. The world around us creates cold-blooded killers, snipers, and other people intent on harming others, and the average person would make the assumption that these people would presumably never stop short of maiming or killing me or my family members for a few dollars.

These people do not have loved ones or friends in their circles, so most think they cannot be steered away from the course of action they have been paid to complete. These unloving and unusually cold people are different but actually easier to deal with than those who have family members to protect and love. Catching a killer is actually easier than catching normal people, because cold-hearted killers suffer from abnormally high levels of paranoia and fear. Once any points of their paranoia or fears are pierced, they immediately feel threatened, fall apart, and move on to other situations and never reappear. When turning the tide on these cold and unloving people, I come after them directly and threaten them by leaving them photos of themselves with simple notes to them, which I have signed. They are used to attacking others from remote hiding places, as that is how they were trained. They stay hidden from their targets and very seldom, if ever, do they meet the individuals or the families of the people they are paid to remove. The problems I pose as a target is that I see everything very differently than they have been trained for, and when people are around, I see their auras very clearly. These auras are much larger than the people themselves, and they radiate visibly outward from any hiding spots regardless of whether it is daytime or nighttime, rainy or sunny. If someone is lurking behind walls, bushes, or in cars, I see them. The challenge is determining quickly if what I am seeing is a threat or not, but I always have the first sight, which gives me an obvious advantage. I can then determine better through direct focus if I have anything to worry about. Once I interpret a potential danger, I take an evasive approach to determine who it is that is watching me. After I figure out who my pursuers are, I approach their world, interact with them from different angles, and ultimately make them uncomfortable by letting them know that I know who they are. Since people are not trained to face the target head-on, they become very nervous and uptight. At this point, I very seldom, if ever, hear from them again.

This night was different though, as I was being pursued with my wife. In the past, they had always hunted me alone, as they were not interested in my family. Very rarely did they threaten my family, and I felt they stayed away from my family almost out of respect. Now, I had the feeling that these pursuers were stepping into new territory, and this time they had intended to create chaos and fear for my wife, almost as though they were saying that the rules of the game were changing and they were tired of playing nicely.

Who were these people, and what did they really want? Did these people have good motivations that would be helpful to others? My immediate assumption was that they were Americans because of the number of people on their team; however, because American clandestine services were not known for coming after family members, I couldn't be sure who they were or the ultimate point of their pursuit of me. This night's events also proved these were very organized trackers, as they were sticking very close to our escape route, almost as though they had mapped out and anticipated our every step—a normal procedure for organizations like the CIA but not usual operational standards for other countries' less sophisticated intelligence services. American intelligence operations had the money to get things done and seldom backed down until the job was finished. So who were they and what did they want from me?

As we were running, I found the place where we could seek cover and told my wife, "Let's stay here."

She looked at the large old building grate and asked, "Do you think this is safe?"

"Yes, they know our route and are waiting, so we have to react differently this time to confuse them."

With that, we stepped into the tight confines and quietly wiggled up the inner cavity until we were about ten feet off the ground.

As soon as we were safely out of sight, we could hear several men run past our location, and after a few more seconds, we could hear several cars pass by as well. Feeling it was safe to whisper, I told my wife, "We need to stay put. These people are good, and good trackers always position others where they believe you'll come out. When you don't show up where you were supposed to, they will backtrack."

She whispered in a concerned voice, which cracked from her being out of breath and on the verge of tears, "Who are they, and what do they want?" She was becoming more concerned. "Do they want to kill us?"

I answered her in a calm voice, hoping to hide my own fears about the situation, "You know what they want; they always want the same thing, but I don't think they want to harm us."

I was trying to make light of the situation and started to tell her, "Let's see if…"

I stopped talking immediately and put my hand over her mouth to keep her from talking as I heard the men return. As they approached our spot, they rattled the grate and looked through its mesh front but never looked up. Our hearts were beating so loudly that I believed they could have heard the intense thumping if they had been quieter.

They had not noticed us and had moved on. I whispered to my wife to stay put, as the danger had merely passed for now, but they would still be looking for us. I told her to stay where she was and that I needed to go out there and track these people to find out who they were so I could start pressing them and making them as uncomfortable as they had just made us.

My wife was calmer now and trusted my abilities. She knew if we were going to be safe, I had to get the information that I was seeking.

I told her, "I will be back shortly, so stay here and don't come out for anyone other than me."

She said, still with a tremor in her voice, "Find those bastards, and come back safely. I love you. Now go get them."

With that, I gave her a kiss and was on my way.

The game of chase was nothing new to me; I had been doing it ever since my visual differences became known publically. Different people from different organizations had always had an interest in using me for their benefit, sometimes for good reasons, sometimes not. Some people or their organizations were simply looking for financial gain, while others wanted to ensure I couldn't use my abilities against their causes. In all cases though, their modus operandi was to seek me out and apprehend me instead of just coming straight out and talking with me. Even though I never feared my own capture, I did worry about my family's safety.

Having grown up with this extrasensory ability, I was provided with a lifetime of education in being crafty and clever in the face of the many different elements and unusual situations that sought me out over the years. Truth be known, I actually enjoyed the chase and enjoyed watching them lose the pursuit. I also believed they enjoyed the process almost as one would enjoy a chess match with a worthy opponent. Since the game had changed in that I now had to look out for the safety of my wife and daughter, I had to manage the game quite differently than I did when it was just me.

Even though my pursuers had never before involved my family directly in these matters, I still always worried for their safety and felt bad for the fear that would engulf them when they found out that I was being targeted. My family is not able to see what I see, so they have to rely solely on my information for comfort and safety. Since they can't see what group or who is after me, they have to live with a fear that never disappears. When someone you love is constantly being stalked and you don't know why or when or have any of the answers, you simply have a greater level of fear. Without the necessary information, you cannot go to the police, the government or family for help because the only way to stop the pursuit is by giving up and joining a group that you don't want to be associated with. To my wife and daughter, this was never fun. Tonight was certainly not pleasant for my wife.

With my wife safely out of harm's way for the moment, I was ready to fight back and start a new game of chess with these guys, whoever they were. I was pissed off at them, not for bothering me but for putting my wife under unnecessary stress. I wanted these guys to learn the meaning of respect and fear and to know I was not someone to be fucked with anymore, so I was on the hunt for the necessary information as to who they were and, more important, who they worked for. Then I could repay their negligent tracking efforts and the terror they had just caused my wife with a little terror of my own.

Before we get too far into my hunt for these people, it's important to describe the depth of my visual differences, as they relate to this story and explain why people were really after me.

Auras to me are not just colored heat waves coming off of someone; I am actually able to interpret things from them. I am able to see the energy levels that are produced by all living—and sometimes dead things if they haven't been dead for too long. When people, animals, plants, and whatever are healthy and happy, they emit a very strong energy level, which I can easily see from far away. These energy levels vary with the person's health, emotions, and mental clarity. The healthier one is, the stronger one's energy levels are and the easier he or she is to see. The stronger these waves are, the more likely they are to emit colors similar to the colors emitted by any instrument of extreme heat or cold. Regardless of whether or not a radiant color is thrown off, the energy levels are always very visible to me and provide me with almost everything I need to know about a person simply with a passing glance.

Most living things have strong energy levels so I usually do not pay much attention to them in passing. When people are sick or mentally impaired, their energy levels become thin or mutilated in some way. This is also a true, although temporary, state of being for people who are in the process of deception or all-out lying.

If someone has a medical issue on a localized part of their body, their energy levels will be weak around the afflicted area. For instance, if someone has cancer in a kidney, that person's energy levels will be very faint outside of the afflicted area. If someone has lost a limb, the body will still present an energy level around where the limb used to be, but it will be very weak. If someone is dying, their entire energy levels are very weak and remain close to their skin. Their body is simply too weak to send off strong energy.

I've always been very low key about letting strangers know I can see this, because responses vary quite significantly. Some people warm up to me with the hope of getting the latest report on their physical well-being, like a sort of medical report or prognosis, while others become hysterical with any news that is anything other than good. Others retreat from me, not wanting to hear about their health from a freak of nature, even though they know the information is correct. Either way, the responses make it not worth the hassle. Many times in my life, I would make the decision to say nothing and live with the pain of what was going to happen to the individuals in question.

Family members and close friends who have known of my abilities for many years and have seen that my predictions and comments are true, accurate, and not used in any way for personal gain have always told me that I have a responsibility to tell others when something is wrong, but I always wonder whether I have that right. An ethical dilemma that I have faced many times is if I know someone is going to die, do I have the responsibility to tell him or her? I've asked myself a thousand times whether I would I want to know if I was going to die. Does this information really help anything or anybody? I came to the personal decision that their lives are theirs alone to deal with, good or bad, and when their numbers are up, they alone have to punch the clock and I should not intervene.

For reasons I've never understood, individuals with mental or physical problems who are emitting low energy levels are attracted to me like metal to a magnet. I can literally walk into any crowded location and immediately become targeted by these people. They become fixated on me and head for me with laser accuracy. I cannot avoid them no matter what tactics I utilize. My family would tell you that I cannot walk through a crowded room, mall, or airport without at least one or two people coming up to me to tell me their whole life story. I spot them at a moment's notice because of their energy levels, and as I identify them, I always turn to my family to forewarn them that these people are in the room and will be making their way through the crowd to speak with me, and they always do.

I have always understood why I can see them and sort them out in a crowd, but what I have never understood is how they can see me. I have never known another person who can actually see the same energy levels that I am capable of seeing. This leads me to believe that everyone can see what I see; they just do it subconsciously for some reason. My friends always refer to this anomaly as a "freak show," because they cannot make any sense of it. They cannot understand why strangers always choose me from a crowd, come directly over, and start revealing their innermost secrets. These encounters have yielded stories of infidelity, personal illnesses, financial troubles, family abuse, and other very dark secrets not readily shared with friends and loved ones, let alone a complete stranger. I must say, I can concur with my friends' comments about this being a freak show because I have never understood the dynamics either. After many years of trying to understand all of the potential reasons only to come up with no viable answers, I have simply stopped asking why and now only work on recognizing who will approach me and figuring out how I can avoid them before they get to me.

When I was a little boy, no one really cared too much about my visual uniqueness; a child's differences are never approached as an adult's are. Often these types of differences in children are scoffed at and toyed with, as though the child is just a newer version of a board game to be actively played by everyone around. As I grew older, the cuteness of my different visual abilities subsided for the adults around me, and curiosity and concern replaced the novelty and fun of my unusual state of being. The problem I was left to face was that no one ever told me when this transition took place or what it really meant.

If no one had been concerned about my oddities, life would have come about normally and I would not have minded at all. I would have bounced through life as carefree as any other person and would never have suspected anything had changed. I actually did so until one major fateful event took place.

The year was 2001, and the United States of America was under attack by faceless foreign invaders; the military needed help identifying these new combatants, and traditional military weaponry was not working. How could our country attack the enemy if they were faceless and, from a military point of view, invisible? How could America defend itself against an invisible enemy? How could the world's strongest military allow acts of terrorism to continue without retribution? How do you defeat a lesser, weaker, cowardly enemy if you can't even recognize or identify them?

My world was about to change dramatically forever, and I had no clue. I would go from being a fun-loving, playful individual without a concern in the world to a person sought after for a perceived birth defect that I had no control over. No one ever told me the best way to prepare for what was to come, and no one could protect me from who would be coming after me.

Before we get to the effects of 2001 and the eventual War on Terror, let's first back up and talk about how this every day, average person with admittedly weird visual abilities became known to the US and other governments as a potential resource—as long as I was on their side. However, if I broke rank and turned against any of the world's governments, I would be looked upon as a threat or, worse, a traitor. How does an average child go from playing tag in the neighborhood with his friends to becoming known internationally as the key figure in "Operation Blur" without even knowing it?

CHAPTER 2

Dead Man on the Park Bench

any people have asked me how old I was when I first started to realize that something was amiss with my sight. I don't really know what age I was when I knew something was different, but I do know my family had to deal with it long before I ever knew anything was odd. I think my differences came to their attention very abruptly with the first significant event being very difficult for them to understand. Because this happened prior to my conscious memory, I have to tell the story as it was told to me when I was much older.

It was a chilly late fall morning outside in our small Chicago suburb. You know the type of weather I'm referring to—cold, damp, and slightly misty so you really can't see too far in the distance. You could smell the heavy air as it wafted along slightly above ground level. Humans were never meant to tread out in the frigid weather that seems to encapsulate Chicago from late fall until late spring. Each year, the inhabitants vow it will be the last time they live in these weather conditions; they promise themselves they will move to sunnier locations in the spring. Yet each year, they return to the challenge and volley with the elements again and again.

I was four years old, and I was being chauffeured to town by my mom in the family station wagon, surely en route to get some necessary supplies like candy or maybe even chocolate milk—a kid's gotta have lots of chocolate milk or he will die. The station wagon I was riding in with my mother was incredible. First, for anyone reading this that is under the age of thirty, station wagons preceded vans and SUVs as the cars of choice for families. These cars had everything: plenty of space to jump around in, seats that folded into many different configurations and could even be made to face backward, tinted windows, auto locks, and in our case, a 455 Pontiac engine that roared even when my mom was driving. I'm positive that the large engine was a requirement of my father's as part of his negotiation with my mother in buying the car. It was a means to overtake the occasional hot-rodder who pulled up alongside of my father and laughed at his ride. The other thing this car had were the first automatic windows ever created for an automobile. Some people might think other cars had this feature before my station wagon, but I tell you, mine was the first car ever to have automatic windows. They were incredible to me, and my job as a typical, average American kid was to test them constantly and make sure they worked perfectly in any weather conditions. A second job that I carried as a kid was to study the effects of automatic windows on parents. When automatic windows hit the market, they did not come with an auto on/off switch on the driver's side that parents could use to prevent a kid from messing with them. My report back to all of the other kids around the nation who had paid me to complete my test was that auto windows were a must and that rolling the windows up and down during cold winter days created the best parental screams. I advised before adjusting the windows in the down direction to make sure one was seated outside of one's parents' backhand reach, which was the auto window on/off switch of the time.

Anyway, there I was, a four-year-old kid on the way to town actively testing my auto window theories on my mom on a very cold day in our Chicago suburb. We passed a park that had some benches located off in the distance beyond the mist, on the far side of the park. I mentioned to my mom that a man was on one of the benches, but he was dead. She was not able to see the man lying down on any of the benches, so she ignored my statement and drove on. I assured her of the man's presence and persisted with my factual observation. I can only imagine what she must have been thinking at the time and am surprised to this day that she didn't drop me off at the nut house.

Even though I was too young to remember exactly everything from this event, my mother has filled in my missing memories to others through the years as she often described how I had taken great issue with her not believing what I had told her as we passed down the road in the distance. According to my mother, I ended my protest by saying that there was really no hurry to go see the man, since he was no longer breathing as a result of his being dead and all. With this comment, my mother looked at me in the rearview mirror. She was concerned, as I was revealing no discomfort or excitability with my observations. Apparently, my nonconforming behavior frightened her, and memories of discussions of my seeing things that she didn't see from the time I was able to speak flashed through her mind, causing her to give in and make an immediate U-turn to head back to the park bench. She wanted, once and for all, to prove to me that I had seen nothing and there was no dead man in the park.

As we approached the man in question, my mother recalled how odd she thought I was for making the remark that the man I saw in the distance had no substantial energy level around him and he was dead. To my eyes there was no blurriness or fuzzy lines being thrown off by the man's body. He was cold and had no energy levels being emitted from his body. He was just plain dead and there was nothing left for me to do but tell the only person within earshot of the discovery. Hence my mother received the news and she had to deal with it however she knew how to. My mother asked herself, as would any sane adult, why would my four-year-old make such a remark? My mother was now dealing with her emotions and was upset because she thought that her son was quite far down the nutty road and in serious need of some mental help. Her fears of how far off from reality she perceived me to be in combination with my callousness and cold assessment of what I had seen had her picturing my future job being the guy that sweeps floors at the local loony ward. She was particularly upset by my saying that the man was dead when she had seen him lying on the bench and she knew he wasn't. She would soon prove to me I was wrong, or would she?

After making our way over to the closest parking spot by the bench, my mother parked the car to give me a stern talking to about the importance of not making up such unfounded stories, especially when it concerned the well-being and feelings of other individuals. Being fairly confused and upset by the anguish I had caused my mother over the matter, I decided she must have been upset with me for the words I had chosen, because after all, the man was still dead from my point of view. So I thought about my words, ever so hopeful that a different use of vocabulary would result in my mother taking care of the situation at hand. With that, I asked her to go home and call the police to come pick up the man. Almost in a state of shock that I would again insist that something was very wrong with the man's state of health, my mother stepped out of the car and walked toward him thinking that she would simply find a man sleeping on the bench and ultimately disprove my assertion forever.

Upon entering the area in the park where the benches were located, two boys rode up on their bikes and stopped suddenly alongside the bench where the man was lying. My mom must have sensed the urgency of the situation, as she could see the two boys' reactions. She ran, holding me by the hand, to see the man. All three of them were staring at him as though he were a mouse in a lab study. There he was with his eyes wide open and mouth agape, a little dried drool seeping out of the corner. He was a little puffy looking, and his skin was a cool shade of blue and his lips purple. And oh yeah, he was dead.

Seemingly from out of nowhere, sirens and flashing lights appeared behind where my mother's car had been parked. An ambulance drove onto the grass toward us, which I apparently thought was cool. I was cheering the driver on as though I was at a stock car race rooting for the winner. What four-year-old wouldn't be excited to see someone drive on the grass? When the police showed up, they began asking a lot of questions, and I guess my mom really didn't know how to answer when they asked how she had found the man. The officer asked her if she knew him. She didn't answer and just continued mumbling out some incomprehensible phrases. The men in the ambulance were busily looking for any signs of life, but even to an untrained eye, it was obvious that the man would not be home for dinner anytime soon. My mother stood beside the bench with her mouth open. Since she was making no sense at all, the policeman asked her to leave. I think she told them everything that had happened, and they just thought she was nuts or in shock, as they couldn't really understand her hysteria.

After the emergency vehicles had left, my mother drove us out of the park and back to our house. It was like she was on a cable that took her directly from the park back to home. My mother drove the remaining distance without saying a word; in fact, I was not sure she was breathing. Speechless, she parked the car and walked into the house. I, on the other hand, was in the same mood as I had been before I saw the man. I was humming tunes as I always did, not to bury any of the scenes that I had just witnessed, but because I had never been able to remember any song verses with the exception of some of the catchier lyrics.

Once I was back in the house, I was less than happy, as I ended up with no candy and no chocolate milk. Damn it, what a crappy way to start a day.

Once inside, I informed her that I was still very hungry. I grabbed her hand and announced that I wanted to get something to eat. Coming out of her fog, my mother looked down at me and for the first time realized that her four-year-old child had witnessed this horrific situation and had come out of it unfazed and unscathed.

Once she finally decided to feed me, I remember the meal she served was not what I was hoping for. The preparations were less than what most enemy soldiers would have been served after they had been captured. I asked my mother the chef why I was being punished with such a meal, but she still didn't speak. My father and brother returned home about an hour later, and I was never so happy to see them. Upon their arrival, my brother and I were sent outside to play in the yard, which we gladly did. When my parents finally allowed us back into the house, I felt like we were playing a detailed game of twenty questions with each question coming back to how I knew the man in the park had died. Later in life, I learned that many of my parents' questions were actually those of the policeman on the scene who made subsequent calls wanting to know how I could see that the man was dead as we were driving by on the main road.

My parents were equally concerned by my laid-back attitude after seeing a dead person. I'm pretty sure they were anticipating that I would someday revert back to a curled-up ball in a mental home after processing what I had seen.

Over time, my parents came to terms with what happened by never discussing it again, with anybody! Children are never any good at softening bad news and can be painfully direct. I was no different, and what I observed was how differently people reacted from any good or bad news. I learned at a young age that children are born without that certain filter that is designed to separate what you are thinking from what actually comes out of your mouth. Every once in a while, I would see a neighbor or friend's pet that had a weak energy level and I would tell them and my family that their pets would soon die. My family and friends never handled this news well. I thought I was doing a great job filtering out by not reporting information that I also saw about the grandparents and even some of the younger adults in the neighborhood who had issues. When the pets passed, most would give my predictions the stamp of coincidence, but when other people's family members passed away after I had warned them their families would swarm around me like I was a direct pipeline to God.

When this happened, my parents would act as though I belonged to someone else, so they could avoid the barrage of questions that immediately started flying around. As I grew, I learned that sometimes it was simply better not to discuss what I was seeing.

Those closest to me recognized that my abilities were genuine. After all of the years of examples and sometimes embarrassing situations that I left them in, they could not dismiss my visual abilities. When I pointed out something adverse was about to happen to someone, they would believe it and try to deal with the news in the most resourceful manner. Such visual tools in the hands of a spiteful teenager who loved playing pranks on others could often prove divisive at best and sometimes deviant. In other words, when my family or friends would irritate me, I would sometimes lob a false visual observation their way to cause them unimaginable fear with which they would have to deal with personally.

I might tell family members they obviously had something wrong with their bodies, because their energy levels were low in a certain area. False observations such as these would send my mother over the top every time. The best part of this was imagining my mother explaining to the doctor why she thought she had this medical condition only to find out there was really nothing wrong with her.

After a few of these experiments, I quickly learned that it was not fair to put others through this kind of anxiety. I really learned my lesson when I told my brother he had a serious problem with the circulation in one of his legs and it needed immediate attention. No one believed me; they all figured I was just angry with him once again. They wouldn't take him to the doctor until one day, his leg swelled to twice the normal size. He needed immediate surgery to remove a large patch of varicose veins; otherwise, he would have had to have it amputated. I also spent many hours in my bathroom sampling the finer tastes of bar soap after giving my family false news.

Still to this day, though my family and friends always ask me how I'm doing when I visit them, they immediately ask me how they are doing as well. What they are really asking me to do is to give them a quick look over to ensure their body is producing strong energy levels. I always tell them the truth unless they are really old, have a known medical condition, or I just don't like them.

CHAPTER 3

Hi, Hippie, My Name is "Bob"

I was just a kid when my family relocated to California. They always claimed that my father's company had transferred him, but I think we moved because my parents wanted a new start where my oddities were not public knowledge. It may also have been because my father never wanted to shovel anymore of that Chicago snow and the California sunshine would help him achieve that goal. Either way, there we were in a new town in a new state, far, far away from whatever it was that we had left behind. If they moved because of me, they should have told me, as I would have played it cool and tried to lay low. I was always truthful to a fault about whatever it was that I was seeing and commented on it directly. Since my family didn't tell me to keep my visions to myself, my mouth started reporting things directly from the moment we hit town. If I saw it, I reported it. That was the case this particular day.

It was a typical hot, dry California day the afternoon the gypsy painted wagon trio pulled into town. The hills were as golden as California's nick-name with no rain in sight. During the summer months, the Californian sun could beat you down into a soul-searching survival fear known only to those who have looked their maker straight in the face and have been left to pray for death as the easy way out. It hadn't rained in months, and no rain was predicted for the near future. The hot summer sun slowed the pace for most people in town, creating conditions under which not much of anything got completed. During those scorching summer days, no one wanted to move let alone work. In those days, the Mexican natives were commonly seen taking a rest, a *siesta*, as they called it, in the afternoon. They wore their sombreros and ponchos as protection from the direct, hot sun while scampering from tree to tree for the shade the trees offered. You could always see droves of these people tucked under any of the town's large, sprawling trees during the afternoon heat.

Although the heat seemed to drain most of the local residents, it usually gave me great energy, but from time to time, it would really piss me off, as I will explain.

The cause for my varying happiness and anger was directly attributable to the heat waves that hovered above the ground on hot afternoon days. Such days have always been very pleasant for me, as they allow my eyes to relax by transforming the heat waves into a constant and very tranquil energy flow. Since birth, I had always been able to see heat radiating off of all living things, part of nature's natural aura. On very hot days, these waves of energy decreased the contrast and the auras blended with it to my eyes. Hot days gave my eyes the opportunity to relax as the auras and radiating heat waves melded themselves together allowing my eyes a break from their normal strain of trying to focus away from the contrasting auras. The best way for me to describe how my eyes see images in life would be to compare it to how people with normal vision see the flowing colors in the aurora borealis. Since seeing energy levels for me has always been my natural state, these hot afternoon heat waves would leave me feeling both energized and thankfully peaceful. However, if there were a situation that caused me not to see the auras, then I would have been very concerned, as that meant what I was seeing was no longer creating an energy flow. As

I mentioned, I see limited or no energy levels when people or things are decaying from disease or age, and this is never a comfortable thing to witness. Others would be uncomfortable and agitated by the heat, but from my perspective, I never thought about the discomfort from the heat too much because of the enjoyment I felt at having a reprieve from my visual differences.

My anger never stemmed from the heat directly, but rather from the indirect repercussions caused by the heat. I was a kid during the 1960s in California, and if you ask anyone who ever lived in California during that time, they will instantly start talking about the hippies. When people thought about California in those days, they thought about surfing, pretty girls, and hippies, which were all synonymous with California at that time. I enjoyed everything that California had to offer except for those damn stinky hippies. I could care less about their desires to smoke their pot, wear those clothes created out of burlap bags and tie-dyed cotton, or have their free sex parties (it should be noted that I didn't know what sex was at the time), and I didn't even care about their crazy music—in fact, I loved the Grateful Dead and would have probably joined the Dead Head movement, but my parents wouldn't take me to the city when I was five. If they had, I probably would have missed my toys; my toys were awesome. Sorry if my digressions are somewhat confusing from time to time, but my friends didn't name me the "Shiny Object Kid" by mistake, as I have the tendency to think about many things all at once.

Getting back to those damn hippies, I can say the two major things I couldn't stand about them was their constant need to say, "Peace, brother," all of the time and their smell, that God-awful smell. My mom bought me a T-shirt with a peace sign on it when I was a kid, and within hours of my receiving it, the fire department had to be called to put out the fire that had unexpectedly caught the garbage can and the garage on fire. The initial cause of the fire was unknown. I can attest though that peace sign hippie shirts go up in flames fast, and they send sparks jumping out so high that early space flight photos are able pinpoint their location.

All was well until the damn garage caught on fire. Who puts garbage cans in a garage with boys around and then gives them hippie shirts? It was my first successful attempt at arson, and I probably would have been hauled off to jail for life had my father not had an understanding as to why I had ignited the shirt. My dad wasn't fond of hippies either. My mother had intended the shirt as a prank gift, but she instantly learned that my position in life was to be endured with strict preferences that could not be negotiated and should not be screwed with. From that point on, I was known as a local five-year-old thug with no respect for hippies. Looking back, I realize I may have overreacted to the shirt, but it sure felt good to be recognized as a five-year-old thug. No one in kindergarten ever pissed off "the Thug," except for when the kids would steal my blanket during nap time. Every once in a while, I would catch them, and as an act of playground vengeance, I would put them in a school garbage can stuffed with paper and starter fluid, but the teachers would always seem to rescue these troublemakers before I could complete their punishment. For some odd reason, it became increasingly difficult to find available trash cans at my school. Damn hippie kids.

The second and primary reason for my hating hippies was caused by their lack of hygiene. These people just plain stank. When you would walk past them on a hot day, their aromas would waft around the area for hours. I always thought it must have taken them hours to get that much stink on them. Your eyes would burn, your throat would start to close, and your stomach would turn for hours. Then they would want to talk to you and say, "Peace, brother."

"Peace, brother? What the hell are you talking about, hippie? You stink like hell, and it's not peaceful to me."

The only thing grosser to me than the smell was the fact that these people were hanging all over each other! Couldn't they smell themselves?

Someone had to tell them they smelled; they had to be informed. So I would let them know about my concern. My mother never really ap-preciated my openness on the topic, as she would always hustle me away from these conversations in a hurry. I never understood why she became concerned, as she always agreed with me later.

That was my five-year-old perspective on life: enjoy the heat waves, but tell the hippies to find a shower and a bar of soap. So, while most people were generally hunkering down in the mid-afternoon sun, I was walking around angrily discussing my viewpoints with the local hippie population.

Getting back to the story, the only thing drier and dustier than the trio's mouths were those of their tattered misfit team of horses and mules, who tugged their ratty wagon. The trio had hopes of finding an end to their aimless, seamless wandering, but their circumstances pointed to a different reality. Onlookers could only feel pity for these lost souls; a helpful solution would have been to give them jobs, but that was never on anyone's mind including the wandering trio's. As I learned later, no one offers vagrant trios work, because people like that don't like work. Instead, the locals always hoped people of this breed would simply disappear and move along to the next town.

In life, I have learned that there is a fine line between unsuccessful situations that create people like this trio as opposed to the successful people on the other end of the spectrum. When successful and unsuccessful people's paths cross in life, it scares the successful people, as they become fearful that this could be them. This reality creates a self-observation so painful that they prefer the people in the negative plight would simply go away. No one had ever explained the fact that even though people wanted these people to move along, they would never come right out and tell them this, as it would be callous and rude. Someone should have informed this particular five-year-old kid, as I took it upon myself to enlighten them of the town's views and tell them to move along. Thinking back to those dark days of direct communications, I have never figured out why I wasn't found floating face down in the local town creek.

This trio had been "a-travelin' hard," as the locals would say. They might not have been hippies, as the hippie movement was new then, but they were either gypsies or vagrants, and everyone knows gypsies and vagrants all became hippies in the sixties, and they all stank equally. They needed to be told to get going, and I felt obliged to inform them of their duty.

When a person has lived in hot conditions, the combination of dirt and spit that lines the mouth can sometimes seem a tasteful meal to the unclean, as was the case with the trio that had just hit town. So foreign were a hot meal and a nice shower for this team that they immediately went about setting up shop hoping to sell some wares and raise enough money to provide them with a fresh start and better their situation. None of them spoke; they just went about business as usual attempting to sell their medical concoctions, knitted and carved handcrafts, and anything else they thought they could use to pry an honest person away from their hard-earned money. The individuals who resided in the small town saw the trinkets the new arrivals displayed as nothing more than junk collected or concocted during their travels. For the most part, there was no intention by the locals to purchase any of the wares except when a passerby felt the need to buy something simply to help them out by giving them some money. I was amazed at how many of the locals would end up paying them simply to be left alone.

Even though this story takes on many similarities to the Old West stories that involved carnies and medicine wagon salespeople, it in fact took place during the late 1960s and early 1970s in California, when society was transitioning from the Old West's ways to those of a new era. The state that would bear witness to some unbelievable greatness, that of innovation, diversity, and the greatest wealth the world had ever seen, would first have to separate itself from its recent past, a past that if not corrected could hold it back from the international promiscuity that would behold its greatness. California was a new land to most, and during the transition from its dark history over the past one hundred years it would have to right some of the wrongs created against others during its early settlement days and statehood days. The days of harassing and killing the Indians, Chinese and other settlers simply for profit or to gain some land would have to come to an end. If California was going to achieve the distinction in years ahead of being the most diverse place on earth, it would have to distance itself from the abuses of the land and rivers inflicted upon it by the inhabitants who arrived during the gold rush days and the industrial boom of the past century.

Being different back then could often cost you everything you owned or even your life. Since I hadn't been educated yet on matters of diversity, and until new training curbed my views, this trio had to be dealt with quickly.

The trio that hit town was in no way atypical to what you'd expect a merchant of the old west to look or act like. They were dirty and wore gypsy-style clothing that matched nothing, including brightly colored trousers with the pant legs tucked into moccasin boots that came up to their knees and were tied tightly with leather ties. Their shirts were all oversized and baggy. The ladies' garters were placed strategically about their elbows to keep the sleeves pulled up as if to prevent the garments from interfering with their hands. The shirts were moist with perspiration and stained at the armpits and neck and beltlines from long days of continuous wear with no washing interrupting their use. The trio's smell was that of defecation and inattention, but the three of them acted as though nothing was odd. Many people would hide their children's faces as they passed by or cross the street to avoid the trio altogether.

When the sheriff arrived, the trio was asked to move on, not because any laws had been violated but because they just didn't fit in. When they refused, they were immediately taken away and their belongings were given away or destroyed along with their animals. By the time they were released, they had no money, no merchandise to sell, and no animals to get them around. Fearing for their safety, the three moved on as best they could under the circumstances.

As a young child, I had inquired of many people as to where they had gone and if they were still alive. I never received an answer and quickly learned that no one cared where they went as long as they wouldn't have to see them or deal with them again. It wasn't until many years later that I learned people don't want to see society's downtrodden, because when it comes so close to home, the realization that it might happen to them is very scary and very hard to deal with for most. Avoidance is the easiest way for most people to deal with the fear.

I was a young child growing up in California in the late 1960s and early 1970s during the hippie period. The country was maturing, and the population was rapidly moving east to west to find the next big opportunity. Companies were moving west; baseball teams were moving west; educators were moving west; doctors were moving west; and people from other countries were moving west. Everyone throughout the world was impacted by this population shift and the opportunities that surrounded it. This was a time when everyone from around the country and the world was looking for the next big fad, the new trend that would transform the world. During this period, California was still new, fresh, and exciting for people who lived in other parts of the world. Hollywood was creating an image of glamour in the movies that would define California. For those who wanted the freedom, the openness, the positive energy that could transform a soul, California was the answer. It was almost like a magical dust had been thrown into the wind by the ancient Indian shamans who walked the Californian soils long ago, allowing California to change the darkest thoughts into bright, open, new philosophical ideas that would transcend the globe. After all, we created IBM, Google, Apple, and the Pet Rock, so we had to be different.

All great things must have a great nemesis in order to stand out—God needs the Devil, pretty needs ugly, Cher needed Sonny, hot needs cold, and California needed the hippies.

Politics had to adjust and embrace the power shift related to the population explosion that engulfed California, or they had to interfere and prevent it from happening. Most politicians recognized the wave as it pushed forward and rode it for all they could get out of it. Growing up in the state with so much going on, I learned how politics really worked, which would help me significantly later on in life. Politics to most voters appears very reactionary, as though people are elected because they are willing to fight for a cause that the people are crusading for. The reality is people only get elected if powerful people want them in office. These powerful people can influence anything they want to happen, and they win, end of story.

One of my earliest memories of using my visual abilities to point me to the truth, a truth the politicians did not share, came when my parents took me to see some of them present their answers to a large audience. I recognized that what they were saying was very different from what they were going to do. They were preaching what everyone wanted to hear, but they were lying. Their energy levels were obviously not in agreement with what they were talking about. At the end of their speeches, I asked my parents why they lied and why everyone cheered. The primary speaker was a soon-to-be president, Richard Nixon, who would later resign. The president's speech didn't bother me as much as the audience's cheering for blatant lies. And this didn't bother me as much as it caused me great confusion. I began to watch political presentations much more closely to better understand why people cheered when being lied to. Since many of the politicians were not being completely dishonest and mostly told the truth, I soon realized that the audiences were cheering when they heard what they wanted to hear, but they were not able to see when someone's energy levels were off because they were lying.

California's needs created the politicians as well as the hippie movement, not by mistake but completely on purpose. At the time, California needed political answers to the problems created years earlier by what had happened to the native Indian tribes, displacement of Mexicans after the Mexican-American War, abuses of the Chinese during the gold rush, the atrocities suffered by the Japanese during World War II, and the release of gay military personnel into San Francisco after the war. But how could politician's best apply their influence properly and be viewed as necessary to the average constituent?

To the world outside of California, the hippies were a fun, free-spirited people, content with creating a new world that included only love and happiness and harmony with the world around them. For those of us who were living in California with hippies in our communities, we knew the truth. The hippie movement was created by politicians so people would elect the politicians to come in and lead the hippies out of California.

These "hippies" were not interested in making the world a mellower place where birds would once again chirp out melodic harmonies or trees would wave in exact concert with one another as the wind blew natural sweet concertos. These hippies were not interested in saving the world or making it a better place. Hippies were just people, just dumb ordinary people too stupid or zoned out on marijuana or other drugs to know or understand they were being manipulated by the politics of the day. But these hippies served to meet a need of the politicians to have something to bitch about and provide a solution for so common citizens would vote for them because they thought they could provide order with respect to these dope-smoking, sex-starved, stinky-ass people.

In summary, if California would have kept the hippies out, we would never have had politicians, and we would have been much better off. A different way of saying it would be thanks to the hippies, California has politicians. So thanks a lot!

Let me back up so you the reader will have a much greater appreciation of the process about which I am talking. Whenever you deal with a population, you have to find a way to control the masses from within their own walls. You can only control a civilization if its population is comfortable. As soon as comforts are depleted, civilization is destroyed. It's a funny thing though, because people always believe civil living and conditions are created and formed by the leaders of the time. The opposite is actually true; civilizations are created and managed by the people, and we allow leaders to manipulate our understanding of the civilization we live in. This manipulation is a long, slow-burning wick that burns over many years or even a lifetime.

The leaders depend on the slowness of the burn in order to systematically carry out their plan. We have all heard the saying that "Rome wasn't built in a day." Also, look at leadership throughout history: Asia has its dynasties, Europe has its kingdoms, and the Egyptians had their pharaohs. Even the United States, as young as this country is, has its share of blue bloods vying for control. Just look at the long family history of the Kennedys or the Rockefellers or the Bushes. These leaders work a lifetime within their family trees to seize control for generations to come. They achieve greatness through the appearance of providing the citizens with the opportunity to live comfortably in a civilized world, a presumptive gift from our leaders to us. *Comfort* is the key word here. As long as the masses are comfortable, then we are contained. If we are contained, then we are malleable, placated, and amenable to whatever is going on around us. We can even be somewhat abused or neglected as long as we are made comfortable in other areas. We've all watched the news and have seen the faces of people living in areas where some great assault has taken place on the local citizens, and we have all said to ourselves, "It doesn't affect me, so all is okay." But what if it did affect you or everyone? Would you still sit idly by and watch unresponsively? This is the game our leaders play with all of us every day. Leaders know they can take advantage of their people as long as they don't anger all of us at once. Do you think having the two political parties in the United States was an accident? Or were they created as a convenience for our leaders, by our leaders?

Leaders have long known that at least two positions of thought must be sustained at all times in order to control the masses. First, by having at least two parties, the population is always split in half. This means our leaders will never have all of us pissed off at them all at once; rather only half will be mad and the other half will be comfortable, so no mass disruptions will take place.

If there was only one political party, then there would be one voice representing the people. When there are two parties, leaders only have to represent 50 percent of the people. When you have two parties, leaders

31

can choose what they want to represent, and at the end of the day, ir-respective of which party the leaders represent, they all have jobs and everything in their world is always fine. They only have to pay attention to half of the population at any given time. Understanding this formula is very important, because in the United States, people are pushing for a third party to represent the citizens. The feeling is admirable, and it seems common sense that if the two political parties we have aren't capable of getting the citizens' goals accomplished, then let's put a third party in that will do as we tell them to.

Be warned though that adding additional parties only reduces the number of people the politicians need to please. For example, if two par-ties exist, then a 51 percent margin is what is necessary to get the vote. If three parties exist, then only a 34 percent vote is needed to get things passed, and our leaders would only need to keep 34 percent of the popula-tion happy instead of the currently required 51 percent; for four parties, the representative number goes down to 26 percent, and so on. So be careful for what you wish for.

Anger and clarity have always been enemies for leaders throughout time. Since the lowest common denominator in civilization has always been the poor, these groups have been the angriest and have always posed the greatest threat to leaders. Just to be sure, there always must be a part of the population that is poor. There can be no exception to this law of physics. However, the definition of "poor" can be very wide. For example, when most people hear the term *poor* they immediately think of the per-son sleeping under a stack of newspapers under a city bridge, in dirty or tattered clothing, not having had a shower or a hot meal in days. This im-agery creates anxiety and fear and is why civilizations have always attacked this issue throughout the years. Leaders know that having too many poor people creates anger, and when too many people are affected, the leaders are no longer creating a comfortable situation.

The reason the "poor" will always exist is because it's a systematic part of the definition of "rich." Imagine if you were worth ten million right now; you would be very rich. Now imagine everyone else in the world is worth one billion; suddenly, you're not so rich anymore. Now imagine you have no money at all, but you have a house, a car, the kids go to a free college, food is free, doctors are free, and all of your luxuries are provided to you for free. You are poor by a monetary definition, but are you really poor? Being poor today in America is much different than it was in the 1930s, and this is what has created our "civilized" state of mind.

To prove that this issue around the definition of "poor" has been around for many years and see what people in the past have tried to do to end it, it's good to look back in history to the Roman Empire. Ancient Roman leaders understood the whole "not in my backyard" theory very well. They knew that most people did not want to see the issues that surfaced as a result of poverty, so they took care of this problem with great zestfulness. The Romans actually demonized the poor and got the citizens to agree that being poor was a crime and the behavior that led to "poorness" should be punishable, and it was. Roman leaders would send troops to the ghettos in the night to round up the poor people to be tossed off the top of the city walls to meet their deaths on the jagged rocks below. Or they were led to the great coliseum and thrown into the spotlight to fight to the death with gladiators and wild animals. If ever there was the motivation to work hard and not be poor, this was it.

Anyway, excuse my digressions and let's get back to the hippies. Leaders have always found distractions to be very helpful, if not necessary, for their own personal causes and political stances. These distractions create opportunities, and when you look back at all of the politicians who have found success in their elections, you will see that they have always been elected for jumping on the right causes and telling everyone they were going to do the things that created more comforts for the greatest numbers in the population. The losers always missed the opportunities to tell the masses the lies they wanted to hear that would make them more comfortable. Instead, they told us the truths we didn't want to hear. As a result, democracy is weakened as time goes on, and eventually, it will crumble if we the people don't do the right things and start bringing in politicians who do what really needs to be done.

So, I knew it was up to me, since everyone just wanted to hear what they wanted to hear from the politicians. If someone was going to be successful in saving California from this hippie invasion, it would have to be me and it would have to start with getting this trio in line. Unfortunately, my mother ended my opportunity to run these founding members of California hippie movement out of town and instead hauled me home where she shoved a bar of soap in my mouth due to my initial outburst to them. My mother alone stopped my march against the new enemy which ended my opportunity to toss this trio out of town and end the hippie movement before it got a stronghold into California. Instead, the Sherriff ran them off and they simply landed in the next town over where they developed roots and created the hippie movement, which in turn created California's politicians. My mom was always quick with stuffing the Ivory Soap bars down my throat anytime I got rolling. I think she actually carried a few extra bars in her purse for emergencies.

What my mother never fully appreciated from my quest was that if my mission had not been blocked and was I successful, the future of California would be altered forever. If these hippies did not leave by sundown, the state would start to bring in all kinds of different people in the future. There could possibly be all kinds of people from all walks of life settling down in our state—gays, Mormons, Middle Easterners, religious fanatics, atheists, animal lovers, people who hate abortion, people who love abortion. Hell, things could get really ugly and the next thing you'd see is a bunch of tech people building a communication system that would allow people from all over the world to show pictures of things and sell things. Finally, our state's politicians would ask to take more money from its people while screwing up our schools, our hospitals, and our children's futures forever. In the end, people with visual differences like mine would be blamed for not telling everyone what they saw when they saw our leaders lying to us all. See what those damn stinky ass, dope smokin' hippies caused! Oh wait, California turned out pretty dang good so never mind.

CHAPTER 4

Decoy

So there we were, hiding from unknown pursuers who had obviously been sent to track us relentlessly. We weren't really wondering *why* they were chasing us around the city, but *who* was chasing us this time? I had been tailed throughout the world by some of the greatest surveillance teams in existence and had become quite used to their processes and habits so this situation, although annoying, wasn't anything new.

These surveillance teams are very obvious after a while, as they all operate with nearly identical mannerisms. I concluded years ago that although these people represent different governments from around the world, they must all get trained by the same teachers, as they go about their tasks in exactly the same way.

The inexperienced person would assume that these people are highly skilled and incredibly intelligent, and their methods of pursuit are very unique. My experience was quite different though, as I always knew when I was being followed and which government body was following me, except for when the US government became involved. The primary difference between the US government and other countries' intelligence groups was that the US government did not back down; they just kept throwing more and more people into the mix until the person being followed simply tired out and eventually gave in to the people leading the chase. The US teams had unlimited resources to get the job done, and they were relentless in their pursuit. Whenever the US teams were involved, I knew it, because of the intensity of the pursuit and their determination to get what they wanted. Since these assailants wouldn't stop, I knew it was the United States that was after me, and I knew my adversaries were not going to let up unchallenged.

Since the level of intensity was so strong, I knew I had to think fast and stay ahead of the game, or I could be in real trouble, I just couldn't immediately think exactly what my best course of action would be to get them to leave me alone.

Other countries' security teams were less well funded and less organized, which always left me with many alternatives for simply slipping away from their grasp. They would eventually give up the chase, probably because other more pressing matters would evolve and occupy their time and resources. The US intelligence groups would never, ever rest. God, these people never stopped! I would run, and they would follow. I would pull some of my usual irritating pranks to add some excitement to the chase, and they would simply be more pissed off once they caught me. They would often express their displeasure about my pranks by beating me up a little, making extreme threats to me, and then leaving me in awkward situations from which I had to figure a way out. You know what I'm talking about, duck-taped to a chair naked in an old abandoned warehouse, strapped to a low-voltage metal chair that would shock me intermittently and hurt like hell, or left stranded in any number of other unpleasant positions. These situations were never fun, and I never looked forward to them, but I knew I really wasn't in any real life-or-death situations, which gave me a glimmer of confidence when being pursued. Since

I knew my capture by the U.S. squads would result in pain, I never liked it when they started following me around. I preferred instead being chased by other countries' teams, because the chase always required a skillful level of logical thought during my flights to safety, but when I was caught, I was rarely beaten, only verbally reprimanded. These non-US countries would give up on me once I started playing some of my usual games, but the US surveillance teams would just keep a tally of my usual annoyances and even the score once they caught me.

I was in Pennsylvania once for meetings for my real occupation when I realized I was being followed. I came up with what I thought was a great solution to the problem and reported the car parked outside my meeting location to the local police. I told them I'd seen the people inside trying to lure young kids into their car. Police don't like grown men who are fooling around with kids, and they were on top of these guys instantly with their guns drawn. They forced them out of their car and made them lie face down on the street as they were roughly cuffed and interrogated. Intelligence agents don't like to have their cover blown, as they know everyone on their team will know they screwed up their mission. So still maintaining their cover, they were hauled off to the local police station to be questioned further.

If this had been one of the international intelligence teams, they would have returned home, a little demoralized, but nevertheless they would have simply left, and the incident would have been over.

Unfortunately for me, it was a US team, and when they woke me from my sound sleep during the wee hours of the following morning in my hotel room, I realized just how pissed they were at my prank. When I woke up, I was very sore, very bloody, and blindfolded. These guys were busy punching me to the sound of each word they spoke.

"You [punch] think [punch] we [punch] are [punch] frickin' idiots [punch]!"

I did think they were idiots, as that was the main thought that circulated in my mind when someone was actively beating my ass, but I felt this probably was not the time to share my thoughts with them. Instead, I took the same evasive actions I took whenever a US team was working me over and played dead. I'd learned how to play dead years earlier while on bear-hunting trips with my father; I learned that it is better to act like you're dead when a bear corners you. Trying to get away from a bear or trying to fight back against a bear only gets their adrenalin up, and they get even more excited and go about harming you further or accidentally killing you.

Since I didn't feel like being killed at the moment, I simply slumped over in the chair that they had me tied to and acted like I was knocked out. Just like bears in the wild, they mauled me a little while longer and then became bored and left me alone. I think they simply got tired from punching me so long. I thought to myself, *You idiots!*

After they had left, I sat there silently with my arms tied and my hood still on for several minutes and listened carefully to make sure they had really left and weren't quietly waiting for me to start moving so they could come over and start beating my ass some more. The only thing I hated more than being beaten was being beaten further for moving around before the abusers actually left, another lesson learned years ago from bears.

After I realized I was alone, I slipped my hands out of the knotted ropes that they had used to tie me to the chair. One of the greatest things that God gave me at birth is small hands and wide wrists; they allow me to get out of jams like this. Once out of the chair, I staggered over to the sink and proceeded to spit out what seemed to be a gallon of blood. I stared into the mirror to take inventory of my body parts. My face was already swollen around the eyes, and my ribs were obviously either cracked or severely bruised, but I still had all of my teeth, neither one of my ears had been cut off, and all of my fingers were still attached. I knew I would be sore for a while, but I would survive to see another day. The hardest part of this whole situation was explaining to the others in my morning meetings how I had been mugged the night before. I had to bullshit people about what had happened that had left me bruised, battered, and scuffed up.

CHAPTER 5

Using All of My Senses

W hen trying to understand how people view the world, it is important to understand their background and upbringing. It is necessary in order to know who they really are. I am no different from others in this world. I am mostly very similar to other people, though a small part of me is unusual and different. It marks my distinction, so I keep those traits hidden from others for self-protection. When you watch others or talk with them in private, you are sometimes able to see a sliver of that small piece that tells who they truly are or what they really believe, but rarely do people ever disclose their deepest thoughts.

I pulled up a chair in the bar and looked around at all of the faces in the room, which was full of people that I had known for many years. I had known their kids, their parents, and even their pets. I could tell you their good and bad habits and if they had been fooling around behind their spouse's backs or moonlighting late-night jobs for some extra cash. Even though I knew so much about the people in this town, I realized I really knew so little about them as people. When they were alone, who were they really? Were they good people, bad people? Were they chasing innocent people around the streets at night, creating chaos for others with the hope of personal gain, or were they the people they appeared to be? How could I know for sure? How could anybody know their real truth?

In schools across the country, we tell our children not to bully other kids. As adults, we feel sorry for the poor little children who are unfairly singled out of the group and ostracized, shunned, and tormented to the point where it is sometimes so uncomfortable for them that they go so far as to take their own lives just to end the pain. I've been both the bully and the bullied in my life, so I understand why it happens and how it happens, and now that I'm older, I only wish it didn't happen. I reflect on these things when I look at others and laugh to myself when I hear new school slogans, such as, "We are going to stomp out bullying." Really? Isn't stomping someone out as a "we" thing bullying itself? "We" can't get others to see the errors of their ways, so "we" are going to stomp them out! Bad ol' bullies. As the spirit of my youthful energy dwindled away and my elder statesmen experiences and wisdom told me that as much as people wanted things like this to change, they never would. As a young man, I wanted to change the world and always heard about those before me who had also tried to change the world only to fail. They would say, "Someday, someone will change things for the better," yet here we sit thousands of years later with the same mediocre schools for our kids, people without jobs, and people without homes while others have everything they want and more…and yes, we still have the bullies.

Statistics show that hundreds of millions of people in the United States alone have died before us, yet what changes did they bring to the world during the time they were alive? As a curious mind, I want to know these people. Were they all people who simply lived in this world for seventy or eighty years and then simply died without making a change, or were they successful game changers in life who achieved their dreams and aspirations of changing the world? Were they big talkers and big goal setters, or were they the world's bullies who achieved success by beating down other people? Did their aspirations cause their kids to look up to them, or did their failures cause their families and friends to look down on them? Did they form armies to invade, bully, and conquer other worlds? Did the invaders' families look up to these people because they were strong, stalwart people, steadfast and resilient in their goals? Did the families of the people being overtaken turn their backs on them in anguish and disgust because they lost these battles, even though they were probably outnumbered by ten to one?

Human behavior is a curious thing; you can study it your whole life and in the end come out wrong because it is always in a flux, and just when you think you understand people, they change. Have you ever rooted for an underdog, and when they win against all odds celebrate the moment, but the next time they are on the stage, cheer against them? Or have you ever rooted for a team to beat another team in sports and been happy when one team beats another? What are your thoughts? I'm usually thinking the losers are pathetic bums. We shouldn't have to see these people anymore after they lose. Their bodies should be tossed over the stadium walls onto sharp rocks below where a solid thud will end their pathetic screaming. Annoying losers!

Napoleon spent his adult life invading countries for gain and profit, nothing else, and he was looked upon as a hero because enough people wanted the same things he did. Hitler wasn't happy being pushed around as a young kid growing up in Austria, and he really used to get pissed off at his father when he was getting the shit kicked out of him as a kid, so when he grew up, he became the bigger bully and kicked the hell out of a whole bunch of weaker people all at once. Hitler and other successful nut jobs from the past and present understood bullying to a level that few people ever do. There is great profit for the bully if handled correctly, but in order to become wealthy from bullying, you have to have a large enough group on your side. We wanted America, so we took it from a bunch of "dumb, lazy natives," who weren't doing anything with the land anyway. We stole people from Africa in the middle of the night and "gave" them jobs in the sugar fields. They were better off though, because in the end, they were provided for as we civilized them. We piss on ourselves, our futures, and what we could become by lacking self-confidence and belief in our own core values to be fair in life. Instead, we try to cheat others out of their money, their homes, and their lives so that we can get ahead. We celebrate the downfall of others because it makes us feel bigger. We also cheer for the underdog, because it is how we all see ourselves. I believe things can change if a group, a region, a country, the world wants it to and has enough confidence to make it happen, but I don't believe the world is confident enough to really want this to happen. Oh yeah, we have to teach our kids in school to stop the bullies, but when they get out into the real world, it's every man for himself as we try to destroy our fellow human beings and then go to our churches, temples, and synagogues to pray for them and ask forgiveness for ourselves.

You really have to laugh at life when you slow down enough to see it. You can look around at everyone and see where they are at in their bullying stages of life. Are they the bully, the person being bullied, or the idle witness watching from a distance hoping life doesn't notice them and does not disrupt their flow? This last group of spineless, non-risk-taking people disgusts me more than stepping in a fresh pile of dog crap in my bare feet at the park. They do nothing to help the people being bullied, as long as they aren't directly affected, but God help the world if they are ever the bullied, because they will whine a river of tears when it's their turn. They will have their non-supporting onlook-ers as well. The one type of people I love and everyone else loves are the rogue individuals who look out for the little guy, the underdog. These are the people in life who operate in the fringes of the legal sys-tems and create their own laws—street laws, if you will—for the good of the common man. These are the people, who break the laws for the betterment of society, and as long as they keep helping the average guy, people will love them, but if they become too big in life, we'll soon hate them as well and send in a new bully to keep life in balance. This is the Al Capone and Elliott Ness saga or the American Revolution chapter or the Billy the Kid story. All the bad guys were breaking the laws of the land in their day in order to stop the bullying. They all stood up and were heard, and history remembers them as both villains and great vindicators.

In all cases, when the bullies get too big, too strong, and too powerful and start irritating others around them, other people bring them down, and this is the circle of life. This is true for individuals as well as countries, and history has proven time and time again that all past great nations have failed because they became too big and too strong, and others get tired of the bullying. America started off with humble beginnings; I just hope we control our bullying desires before our ego gets the best of us and destroys the greatest nation in the history of the world. It's good to know though that if readers disagree with me on this, I will personally come to your house with a bunch of friends and we will kick your ass, unless of course you and your friends are bigger, then we will discuss why you shouldn't bully us.

I thought back to the past evening when my wife and I had to hide from pursuers during a rainstorm and laughed to myself. Now, I was in this bar, this smelly, stale bar that I had been in a thousand times before, with its dirty top shelves and antique jukebox that hadn't had any new music added since the 1980s but still blared the old hits the same way it had done decades ago. The people were the same as they were in the eighties, too, just older, balder, and more wrinkled. The lights in the bar that worked were dim as though they were barely hanging on to life. The bar had its own odor, kind of a rain-soaked leather smell combined with years of cigarette smoke. It didn't smell like the people who were visiting, but rather caused the visitors to smell like itself—a kind of souvenir for everyone who visited, as though it was acting, and giving off its smell was its role in the play.

I had visited the bar, which was now filled with these older people whom I had known for many years, many times, and this night, after thinking about the other evening's events, I realized these people, old friends really, didn't know anything about who I really was either. As I sat at the bar that evening thinking about being chased and thinking about how easily we escaped our potential captors, I started to laugh to myself, out of control and almost hysterically. Then I felt my hand, which was still holding my evening's drink, start to tremble violently, as I feared for my wife, thinking how real the situation was and how real it could have become.

If someone came up to you and asked you to reveal your most desired fantasy, could you? I know most people immediately go to thoughts of being the president, owning the bright-red Ferrari, getting a date with the hot-looking blonde up the street, and so on, but I'm talking about real, deep-seated fantasies. I am talking about fantasies of substance or life-changing experiences. If I had been born deaf, I would wonder what it would be like to hear. Would the world be different if all of a sudden, the sounds reverberated in my head, leaving me with the ability to recognize my surroundings better? Would I spend all of my time chasing the creatures and machines that created the new sounds? Would my other senses that had guided my world prior to my new ability become less necessary or numb? How would the world really change for me? Would I actually be nervous because of my new ability to hear, and would this new confusion cause me to wish I could return to the simpler world that I had been accustomed to when I was deaf?

What if I had been born without the use of my legs or arms and suddenly, as if by magic, modern medicine came up with a solution for me that provided me with new limbs? How would this change improve my situation? Where I would have always wondered how it would feel to walk, throw a ball, run, ride a bike, or pet a kitten. Would my new limbs create a sense of enlightenment, or would they simply cause me to experience the overstimulation felt by others? Would my simple world, as it would be viewed by other "normal" people, all of a sudden become more complex?

Would the complexities of being "normal" like others with arms and legs create new risks for me or cause me to fear? Would I also have to change my goals and daily habits to those of the other "normal" people in order to deal with my new limbs? Would others stop treating me differently and stop offering to help me, and would I be okay with this since I'd been looked at as being handicapped up until that point?

If I were an orphan, I would wonder what it would be like to have a family. As an orphan, I would be independent and would not have to worry about others. People look at orphans with a heavy heart and wonder how a parent could do this to a child. As an orphan, would I feel left out by life? I wouldn't have a brother or a sister or parents or grandparents, but I also wouldn't have the worries many others suffer in typical family situations either. I wouldn't have a drunken parent abusing me or a sibling with whom I would have to share toys. I wouldn't feel bad when a loved one passed away. I wouldn't live the anguish that one feels when a family member has to move for a job or loses a job. I wouldn't miss the love of other family members. If I had been an orphan, I would have only myself to worry about. I would be stronger, more capable of dealing with a tough, sometimes challenging world. So would being adopted change my world and cause me emotional problems or leave me in a state of paranoia that the new family wouldn't accept me for who I was? So would a kid be better off being left alone as an orphan or as an adopted child?

The further the normality is away from most people, the greater the fantasy. People are mostly good by nature and try to make things better for those less fortunate or not "normal." The average person is not able to understand how others "less fortunate" than him- or herself can get through life with such disadvantages. When people see something unusual or foreign to what is considered normal, they act out to try to change the situation or to eliminate it because of the dark fear that they too could find themselves in the same situation. This is why when we see bums begging, we either try to help or become angry with them. This is also why bullying exists at many levels, not just in our schools. Seeing something ugly or scary reinforces humans' need to help or eliminate things. As people, we can't simply ignore the concern or fear, because we are all so close to the deep, dark worries that come about from what we are seeing.

As I grew and came to understand that I saw the world differently from others, I began to wonder what it would be like to see the world through another person's eyes. Would the colors that I see be the same as what he or she sees? Is the sky others see bluer than my eyes lead me to believe? When it's dark outside, can others see the animals that I see, or are they hidden in the darkness? Is this why some people are scared of the dark and others show no fear of it? Are race-car drivers able to see the world more clearly at high speeds, while others can't drive at these same high speeds because their vision can't focus at such velocity? Why did my eyesight develop differently? What other senses did I lose as a result of my differences?

Experts over the years have told me my sight differences were a "disability" that was probably caused many years ago by head trauma. If my eyesight was a "disability," then why did my closest friends rely on it through the years, and why was the government seeking to understand it and use it for their needs? I have never felt I had a disability as a result of my visual differences, and in fact, if no one had ever labeled it as a disability, I wouldn't even have felt different. I raced motorcycles for many years when I was younger and had several spectacular accidents that went hand in hand with that sport, so oftentimes; people suggested the probable cause of the head trauma that created my visual differences was from a motorcycle accident. People have always tried to link my visual difference with a cause. As I noted before, people try to "help" or simply understand why things become what they become; everything must have a logical answer. Blaming my difference on accidents isn't valid though, because I didn't race from the time I was born, but I have had my vision differences since birth. I should point out though that I must have had severe brain issues to start racing in the first place, because although I know the sport never caused any changes to my vision, it was very dangerous. I'm really not sure why I ever gravitated toward it to begin with. Even more inter-esting to me is the fact that if someone gave me the opportunity to ride their motorcycle in a race today, I would excitedly accept it.

Regardless of what everyone around me concluded about my visual differences, the visual differences that I was born with were anything but a disability, and as time would prove, my differences would become very useful and fortuitous. Although they were sometimes challenging and led me to feel like a science experiment or an exhibit in some freak show at the circus, they were an incredible tool for many reasons, and it was up to me to utilize them to the best of my ability.

Realization of being different isn't bestowed upon people at birth au-tomatically. You don't just wake up one day knowing something is amiss. The realization is slow, and the difference is often recognized by others around you first. Many times, the acknowledgment is not fully made until much later in life by a spouse or children. From the first time that I ever started playing with other children and interacting with adults, animals, or inanimate objects, I was always able to identify what was safe to play with and what was not. I can remember walking up to large dogs, petting them, and playing with them from the time I could walk, much to the surprise and concern of the adults. I never had a fear of a bad out-come, because I knew by the animal's energy levels that I was never in any danger. Animals big or small with strong energy levels were always calm and never meant any harm. This held true for cattle, horses, dogs, cats, and people. When playing with other children, I could immediately tell which children I should play with and which to avoid. Boys will be boys, and boys start to try to distinguish early in life by fighting with other children. These challenges for fights always caused me great con-fusion, because most times, when other boys would engage in activities that would result in a fight, I could tell by the tightening or thinning of their energy levels that they really did not want to fight and they were very nervous and uncomfortable to be in the situation they were in, even if they caused the chaos. They were simply trying to fake the other person out through intimidation in hopes that the other person would simply walk away.

It was my engagement with these individuals where I gained the most respect from my peers. As soon as I saw the thinning of their energy levels, I knew instantly how scared they were regardless of their size, and I could easily surmise that they just wanted the situation to disappear. Knowing their fear levels, I would take an aggressive approach toward the fight, and they would always back down. These children would never approach me again to fight, and my reputation grew as a result. For the children who wouldn't back down, their energy levels would always tighten just before they were about to strike me, so as soon as their energy levels changed, I would always throw the first punch to surprise them. If their energy level stayed tight, I would not strike them again, because I knew their fear would overpower their desire to fight. For those who had strong energy flow after my first punch, I would keep punching them until their energy levels tightened.

If I was to leave you thinking that a visual difference only helped me defend myself from other children, it would be a disappointingly short story. The best way to illustrate the value of this added sensory ability would be for me to ask someone who had never been able to smell, see, hear, or touch to define what it would be like to perform those natural activities. They couldn't, because sensing is an activity that your body participates in every day of your life at many different levels. If you have never had sight, you could not describe having these sensory results. People who have sight usually feel sorry for those born blind. "How awful it must be not to be able to see the colors of the rainbow, the sky, and your children" is a common remark made by those who have sight. The blind person though doesn't know what he or she is missing, so they don't miss it. Also, blind people's other sensory abilities are greatly enhanced by the lack of sight. Have you ever seen a blind person walking down a busy city sidewalk during rush hour and thought, *Oh no, they'll be killed! Someone needs to help them!* And then while you watch them continue on their way, you notice they don't need any help at all. This is because of the magnification of their other senses. They typically hear better, identify more using touch and smell, and are in no way derailed by their difference in vision.

My senses are in most ways exactly the same as other people; I just have an extra thing. When people ask me what it's like to have this extra "ability," I just laugh. I don't have an extra power; I can't fly, can't jump buildings, and can't shoot webs out of my arms. I also believe there is a balancing force that equalizes people with one another. In other words, most geniuses are not able to speak simple sentences. Most people who are somewhat mentally slower than average people have an incredible level of "street smarts" and are capable of doing very well in life.

I know my other senses are somewhat lessened by my having this extra sense, just because of the fact that with this added sense, I don't have to rely on my other senses as much. So it all balances out with everyone.

This gives me an opportunity to help others understand that the world is not viewed in only one way, and though one person may see the world a certain way, most likely, others see it in many different ways.

I think I learned about the most interesting phenomenon associated with my vision for the first time when I was in my late twenties; I discovered that when most people read books, they see the letters outlined by the white space. I view writing just the opposite; I see the missing letters cut out from the white space and identify them that way. This actually gives me an advantage when speed reading because I can instantly identify the missing letters while most people have to read all of the letters in sequence and identify what has been added to paper.

To me, it's no different than someone looking at a block of Swiss cheese, and some people saying they see the holes while others see the cheese.

My wife currently was not trying to figure how I was looking at the cheese though; she was asking me how the hell we were going to get out of the particular mess that we had found ourselves in. She was very curious as to who this was that was after us and why and would like to spend more time later reviewing the facts, but only after we were out of the rain, out of the shadows, and in the safety of another place, anywhere but where we were now.

CHAPTER 6

School, Sex, and Bigfoot

Kids in junior high and high school always confused me by the difference between their actions toward the opposite sex and what their auras were showing me. Many of my friends who dated one another could be heard saying how much they loved each other and that they would stay together forever. I always hated that emotional crap back then, because it sounded so pathetic and I knew from what I was seeing that it was nothing more than a bunch of BS. I used to chuckle to myself whenever I would hear the *love* word because what they were saying to each other and what their energy levels conveyed were usually very different. Most of my buddies would exhibit a high energy level whenever any girls came around, and most of the girls I knew exhibited even higher energy levels around guys other than their boyfriends.

It was really funny when one of the couples was in each other's arms and another person arrived on the scene. They would act out all the proper etiquette, but their energy levels would reveal completely differ-ent desires. I would ask my friends why they kept dating each other when they obviously wanted someone else. They would completely discount my questions and deny any improper feelings they had outside of the relationship. My closest friends started out skeptical of my ability to see these trends, but once they understood I was right in my assertions, they would confide in me their true thoughts about their relationships. This was the first time in my life that I started to recognize that others might not be able to see the world the way I was seeing things. My friends usually classified my interpretations as merely an ability to follow a hunch about people. Some of my friends even would go as far as to say that I had a really strong ability to understand women, but the truth was I was seeing their real feelings because of what their auras' energy levels were telling me. I can assure you that even though I had this extrasensory gift, I still was unable to understand girls any better than anyone else.

I would say to myself, *Me understand women?* Wow, were my friends clueless. At that age, I didn't know how to operate most kitchen or restroom appliances, let alone understand women. In fact, its thirty years later now, and I still don't understand women. Life hasn't been a complete waste for me though, because I can operate a toaster without supervision and I am also happy to report that after almost twenty years of marriage, I have learned what that little flipper handle is on the side of the toilet. However, I must admit that I am much happier now that the automatic public toilets have eliminated the need for the flipper handles.

Sorry for the detour, my brain does that a lot, and I go off on tangents. It's like what happened when I was with my father in the Olympia National Rain Forest in Washington State years ago for a bow-hunting trip. Anyone who has ever hunted using a bow knows the drill. You put on as much camouflage clothing as possible to stay warm because you'll be sitting in a tree stand all day. No matter how much clothing you have on, it's never enough, and you'll freeze all day. You won't freeze to death though; that would be too easy. You'll only freeze right up to the point of death, but you'll survive just long enough to catch pneumonia. The reason you'll be so cold is because it's a known fact that there has never been a hunting trip where it hasn't rained or snowed the entire trip.

The hunting rule book says it must rain hard enough for the water to soak you through all the layers of your protective clothing and reach your skin. Only once you are soaked thoroughly is the snow allowed to start. Snow on a hunting trip serves only two purposes. First, it is designed to freeze your already soaked clothing. Second, it changes what everything looked like when you entered the forest. The snow is magnificent at covering the trail markers you set coming into the forest. Once the trail markings are covered, you will be thoroughly lost for several more hours to ensure you become sick enough to actually say you were on a hunting trip.

Hunting boots must also be worn to ensure they fill up with enough water while hunting to freeze your toes off. It's common knowledge that when a forest ranger happens upon people in the forest who claim to be hunting, the ranger will ask these people to remove their boots and show proof of their toeless, nubbed foot stumps. If they take off their boots and they have all of their toes, it proves they are not hunters at all and they are immediately arrested. Many photographers and ruthless bird watchers who pose as hunters are captured this way.

The final preparation that was always applied right before an archery hunt was a heaping amount of skunk oil. Yes, skunk oil. Apparently, humans smell worse than skunks in the forest, so adding a little skunk perfume would bring the animals closer to us. With guidance like this, is it any wonder I didn't understand women? A side note worth mentioning here is skunk oil can be purchased at any outdoors store and is a must-have when you feel like playing a prank on any of your friends. It's also helpful to know that when body temperatures rise, so does the level of the skunk oil aroma. So if you opened your friend's locker and dripped a drop or two into his shorts, he would become somewhat embarrassed after he started sweating in the gym clothes.

Anyway, my father and I had set up our tree stand and were ready to wait out our prey. It was always boring as hell. The first time I was ever in a tree stand, I was afraid I would fall asleep and roll off and die. After several hunting trips, my fear changed, and I was afraid I wouldn't fall off and die. In fact, my father never could figure out why I would always put sharp objects under the tree stand; I was just ensuring that if I fell out of the stand, I would land on the sharp objects below to my swift death. I didn't want a slow death, just a quick one would do.

Now let's get back to the story of the Olympia National Park trip. My father and I had been out all day in a typical rainy, snowy day when I saw something in the distance. I whispered to my father, "Dad, look over there! I think a bear is coming toward us."

He couldn't see it yet, as it was too far off in the distance. His response to me when I saw something that he didn't was always one of mentorship and guidance from a father to a son. "Shut up, dumbass. There's nothing out there."

Since I was only seeing the energy levels it was emitting, I couldn't tell him what it was, but it sure looked big. Just another side note, the best way to understand what energy levels look like is to imagine you're driving down a long highway during a hot afternoon. When you look into the distance, you can see the heat rising off the road giving a foggy or blurred type appearance. That same wavy fog look is how I see energy levels on people, animals, and all other life forms. Because of this ability, I often see the energy far earlier than the object emitting it.

This was the case with what I was seeing now. It was starting to become dark, which helped my vision, but hindered my father's. We stayed as quiet as possible so our stinky skunk-oil-covered frozen bodies could do their magic. As the object came closer, my father whispered, "It's another hunter."

I whispered back to him in my typical smart-ass way, "If it's another hunter, we should probably put a couple of arrows in him to put him out of his misery."

My dad never appreciated my subtleties or my sense of humor, but I always thought I was funnier than hell. The object came closer yet. We were both seeing it clearly now, but we couldn't figure out what we were actually seeing. Was it a bear or a man? It was now within thirty feet of us, and we still couldn't tell. It walked straight up like a man and had a huge upper body, but it also had long hair like a bear. I thought it was just another one of those damn hippies, so I told my father, "I'm going to shoot him."

My father informed me it was against the law to shoot hippies out of season. Damn rules and damn hippies! Whatever this thing was, it also had the most noxious smell that I had ever encountered. This was the first time I understood why putting skunk oil on was helpful for hunting: if the animals smelled us with our skunk oil on and then smelled this thing, we would win the pretty-smell contest.

The man or animal finally stood directly below us. My father and I were completely dumbfounded as to what we were seeing. I knew we would be stuck in that damn tree though if it didn't leave soon, and all I wanted to do at that moment in time was get back to the dry car and turn on the heater. So I did what any fifteen-year-old would do, I poured my soda on its head. Later that evening, my father informed me that my mother had actually had an affair early on during their marriage and I wasn't really related to him. He said he couldn't prove it, because they didn't do DNA testing back then, but there was no way something like me could have descended from his loins.

Well, whatever this smelly thing was, it was not as happy as it had been earlier after having soda dumped on its head. It grabbed hold of the tree and started to rock it back and forth, snarling the whole time. Now I ordinarily, wouldn't have minded the rocking of the tree since I had always tossed things out of the little tree back home onto my brother's head, and he would always respond by trying to shake me out of the tree. What concerned me here was the tree we were in was a rather large redwood tree and this thing was managing to shake it rather well. I responded by telling my father, "You should climb down there and discuss the situation at hand with this thing and see if you can come to an agreement."

Again, my father mentored me for my remarks. "Shut up, sit there, and hang onto the tree." Even though we both had our bows, we knew not to dare shoot this thing because it was much bigger than any bear we had ever seen and the only damage we could do was make it angrier. So we held on and waited for it to leave, and it eventually did. We were lucky that this thing didn't climb trees, or we would have been stuck. As the thing walked back into the forest, my teenage humor trickled through my brain, and I asked my dad, "Should I put an arrow in its ass as it is leaving?"

My father's response was a silent stare, but I knew what he would have said if he had not been shaking too much to speak: "Shut up, dumbass."

We never did figure out what exactly it was. I did know one thing for sure, whatever it was, it was an older brother because the way he shook that tree sure reminded me of my older brother when he was angry with me.

My father never liked to believe in my vision differences when I was younger. Whenever my mother or friends wanted help finding a stray animal in the dark, they would ask for my help, but my father would derail the entire conversation anytime the subject matter came up and exclaim that I just had very good night vision. I can count on one hand how many times my father ever asked me to use my skills for his personal benefit, with the exception of when he asked me to help him win poker games, and this was one of those times. He would not come down from the tree stand until I was no longer able to see the energy levels from the thing that had paid us the visit.

By then, it was pitch-black outside, and my father was now dependant on my vision. He wanted to know everything that I was seeing on the way back to the car. He asked me at least fifty times, "Do you see anything?"

I would say, "No, I don't see anything," becoming angrier and angrier each time he asked the question. Finally, after he'd asked me enough times to really piss me off, realizing how numb my feet were as we walked, I finally exclaimed, "No, I don't see anything, and I can't feel my fucking toes anymore either because this stupid trip caused them to fall off!"

When I swore, my dad yelled at me and asked why I talked like that and who I'd heard say such foul words. I'd heard them from him, my uncle, my brother, the kids in the neighborhood, and even my preacher once, but that was understandable after the prank that I had pulled on him. Poor old preacher, I think he's still in therapy and not expected to fully recover. I thought I shouldn't answer my father's question about the swearing and felt I should just ignore it all and get us back to the car.

We had our flashlights, so we could navigate the darkness and get back without too much difficulty. It was unusual for my father to be as alarmed as he was. We had come upon many bears and other aggressive animals during hunts in the past, but this was different. My dad wanted no part of this thing or this trip any longer. We left the tree stand and most of our supplies back in the tree. The only things we took out were the bows and arrows, the flashlights, and of course, I took the remaining skunk oil. On the way back to the car, I only saw a couple of little energy balls, most likely a family of raccoons and one big energy ball, which moved like a deer. When we made it to the car, my father got in and took off faster than I'd ever seen him move. He didn't talk much while driving for the first hour or so, and then when he started talking, he couldn't shut up. In the end, he vowed never to discuss what we had seen, and he held true to that vow until his dying day when right before he passed away, he murmured out to the family all that he had seen and experienced in life. His very last comment was, "I saw Bigfoot!"

So, let's get back to my friends' dating rituals. Remember, I have a tendency to drift from time to time. I may have been blessed from birth with unusual eyesight, but I wasn't blessed with a strong sense of focus while telling stories. My buddies started to realize that my gift of vision was more than an ability to understand women; I was actually able to see when the girls had an interest in one of my friends or when she didn't. My friends started to rely on my vision more and more, as they knew I could tell when a girl was angry, uninterested, or scared. Low energy levels are a reflection of someone being tense. High energy levels indicate comfort. When my buddies were interested in someone, they could find out if the feelings were mutual or if they were wasting their time by asking me.

At first, it was fun sharing what was happening, but then I started to recognize things going on around me that made me extremely uncomfortable. There were times when some of my friends' girlfriends would have very strong energy levels around my other friends. For obvious reasons, I would not want to report what I was seeing. It then became a no-win situation, because my friends would ask why I hadn't warned them that the girl was becoming interested in someone else.

During my high school years, I noticed that the guys' and girls' auras changed quite quickly, indicating that their attention was shifting between people very often. It would even shift back to someone they had had an interest in previously. It was very interesting to me because happiness followed the auras. If two people shared the same aura intensity, when they were around each other, they were as happy as could be. Once one of their auras shifted to someone else, their intensity changed, and they would stop getting along as well. Once their auras were showing moderate attraction to each other, they would get along better than when one of their auras was fading, but the relationship was only friendship. They couldn't hide their feelings with what they were saying with their auras, and I knew when to hang out with them and when to stay away from them if I didn't want to deal with their drama as a result.

An unexpected problem surfaced when I was a senior in high school and one of my closest buddies started hanging out with a new friend. Energy levels have never presented themselves to me incorrectly. All my life, energy levels revealed who liked whom and who was comfortable with whom. Girls have a tendency to let down their guard more than boys do and are genuinely more affectionate than boys. In general, they possess much stronger energy levels. Often girls are harder to read, because it's difficult to understand where their comfort levels stop and their compassion levels begin. This also makes it more difficult to tell if a girl is interested in another girl. Boys, on the other hand, never become fully comfortable around other boys unless they are being submissive. Growing up in California, I saw homosexual behavior at an early age, and I learned about how the energy levels worked in those situations. Now don't get me wrong here, I don't care if people are homosexual, heterosexual, bisexual, or whatever; I'm simply reporting what I saw going on. Personally, I like women for many reasons, and that will never change, but I have friends from all walks of life and really don't care what they are as long as they don't try to push it on me.

Anyway, my buddy and his new friend were hanging out a lot, and I could see what was happening, but my buddy couldn't. His new friend was much more interested in him than he was in his new buddy. What was I to do? My buddy would kill this guy if he figured out what was going on. So I did the wise thing and did nothing. What I had learned was the less I said, the better; things would work themselves out. My buddy never killed the guy, and they are still friends today. My buddy has his family, and his friend lives with his friend in the city.

When my friend asked me years later if I had noticed anything with respect to his friend's aura that could have forewarned him of the situation, I told him, "Yes." However, I told him there was no way I was going to say something that could have caused a really big issue for both of them at the time; so instead, I opted out of the whole thing. My buddy was not happy with me for not saying anything at the time, but he understood why I didn't. I hate to say it though; he'll have more issues to deal with like this, because what he doesn't know yet is his daughter is definitely attracted to other females.

Although this ability helped my dating life throughout the years, it also caused me great angst, because sometimes, when I wanted a relationship to work, I could see right away that it wouldn't. The major lessons that I learned from my abilities came in college when I tried pushing the limits on what I was seeing from the energy levels by asking girls or their friends many questions. I learned that most people are afraid of what they know to be true, and they usually do not want others to know their true feelings. I have never been slapped so many times in my life. So the main lesson I learned from all of this is to sit in quiet observation and reflect on my own thoughts and never, ever discuss what I'm seeing with others.

CHAPTER 7

Mixing It Up

While in Chicago for another business trip, I stopped in one evening at one of my favorite sports bars for some dinner, a beer, and to catch up on the day's baseball game scores. Since I was born in Chicago, sports are hard wired into my DNA. As anyone from Chicago will attest, there is no better place on the face of the earth than Chicago for sports fans. New York has the Yankees; Boston has the Red Socks, Celtics, and Bruins; LA has the Lakers; and Dallas has "America's Team," but that's all they are, just teams. Chicago, on the other hand, is a city that is built for sports, and it is a way of life. The main difference is most of the restaurants are named after and have meals named after local legendary players; hotel rooms are dedicated to great players who stayed there; and kids are nicknamed "Sweetness," "Mikita,'" and "Butkus" after the champions who wore those names on their jerseys. School awards are named after these local hometown heroes to signify the high level of accomplishment that the kids have achieved in winning them.

In Chicago, athletes achieving excellence in sports would be considered super achievers; in other, lesser cities, the mark is not set to the same standards, but in Chicago the standards are so high that great achievers are average and only those who achieve the rankings of super-human status show up in the towns' archives. Players like Pippen, who is arguably one of the best basketball players to have ever donned a uniform and would have been the top on any other team in the country, was instead merely a shadow to the greatest legendary player in the history of basketball, Michael Jordan. Athletes like "Iron Mike" Ditka, Gayle Sayers, Dick Butkus, and Walter Payton didn't simply play ball in Chicago; they bled for Chicago. Chicago is a city where they celebrate the human being who wears the uniform and not only if they win their respective championships. They respect the people, and the great ones return their respect to the people of Chicago by playing with sheer grit and leaving everything they have out on the floor. Don't believe me? Ask anyone in Chicago who the late Brian Piccolo was, and they will tell you. Brian was too small and too slow for football, but he played with grit for the city he loved and was a winner until the day he died.

This city doesn't care what your background or upbringing was; it only cares about what you will become when you put on that Chicago jersey, like Halas, who was spawned by Bohemian immigrants and formed the Bears at a meeting in Canton for one hundred dollars. Other early sporting visionaries, such as Marshall Fields, George Pullman, and Philip Armour, made sports a reality for Chicago by funding the movement. Late great commentators, such as Harey Carey, with their voices, painted visual images on the minds of everyone who listened to the games they were calling. Their voices still resonate in the wind that blows over the city today.

If you don't know your sports history in this town, you may go hungry and end up sleeping out on a park bench, and trust me; this is not a city where you want to do that.

So there I was stopping at one of my favorite sporting digs in the city hoping to get a beer and some ribs while catching the evening scores, when in through the front door comes a familiar face. He was followed by two other guys. It was one of the US intelligence team guys I had pulled the prank on while in Philly and undoubtedly one of the guys who beat my ass in my hotel room the next morning. I couldn't be sure if he was the guy who had worked me over because they had a sack over my face, but if I were a betting man, which I am, I would bet quite a lot of money that I was correct in my assumption.

In any case, he looked straight at me and winked as he walked toward me. The two other men with him waited at the front door and looked around as though they were waiting to meet someone else. These two guys were huge, and I knew two things right away: I was no longer hungry, and these two guys would soon be working me over if I didn't play their game, whatever that was. As a form of habit after dealing with these types of encounters for many years, I never let anyone simply walk up to me without having some plan for defense or divergence. Out of habit, I always took one of the extra forks on the table and laid it in my lap, just in case. I always used a fork and not a knife, because people notice when knives are missing but they never notice absent forks. Also, forks work better, as they leave multiple punctures, and knives only leave one hole. A fork in the proper hands is simply a terrifying experience for the person being stabbed with it.

The man sat down at my table and began to speak with me. Instantly, I recognized his voice as the voice of the guy who had beat the hell out of me in Philly—I didn't like him. He proceeded to tell me the service was tired of these cat-and-mouse games with me and it was time for me to stop playing around and get serious. I had to join up, or my next beating would not have as happy of an ending as it did in Philly. He continued to tell me that life in the intelligence service was a good one, and the people I would be working with were also good people. I would be doing my country a great favor, as I could help with intelligence interrogations. While he was talking about all of the good people I would be working with, all I could think about was all of the "good" people who had chased me around the world and some of the really "good" people who had used me as a human punching bag.

Now don't get me wrong, I love my country and fellow Americans more than anyone, but I'm not a big fan of some of our government recruiting programs and I didn't much care for this guy's tactics. I still felt like I owed him from our last meeting, so I acquiesced to his speech by telling him I would join under the right conditions and would require a meeting with someone else. I knew I had to give him a positive to take back to his superiors; a "no" answer would have simply reacquainted me with a beating from the two cronies standing guard at the door.

He seemed very relieved by my response, as his permanent scowl replaced itself for a split second with a crusty smile. He had accomplished his job of getting an affirmative response from me, so now we could be friends and I could eat in peace.

Never for a second during this exchange did I ever forget our last meeting, nor did I forget how public the forum we were both seated in was. So I asked him, "When you were beating me up in Philly, why did you let me live?"

He replied, "I had my orders."

I rebuffed, "But you wanted to kill me."

His response was interesting. "I don't question your abilities, but I don't like being played for a fool or embarrassed in front of my team. When I realized what you had told the cops in Philly, I kind of respected your move, but I still wanted to eliminate you because you have always been a royal pain in my ass."

In order to set the record straight, I had him acknowledge one key point. "You know it was you who started harassing me, and I never wanted involvement with your team."

"Yes. So?"

With that, I clenched the fork in my lap and slammed it down through the back of his right hand as it rested on the table. The tines of the fork went straight through his hand, pinning it to the wooden table.

"Oh, son of a bitch!" he yelped.

With his hand still stuck solidly to the table, I told him if he ever threatened me in any way ever again, I would personally remove his right hand myself.

"What the hell do you have against my right hand?"

"When you were beating my ass in Philly, I noticed you were right-handed, as those punches hurt the most."

Seeing that his two thugs were making their way quickly over to my table, I told him to pull the fork out, take his hired help with him, and go give his superiors my answer. I also told him to get his bloody hand the hell off of my table, as it was making a damn mess on the tablecloth.

He stood up, wrapped his hand in a napkin, and motioned for his guys to stay put. He then turned back to me and said, "You either have guts or you're as dumb as a horse. Either way, someday, you are going to make a huge mistake and end up dead in the street, and I hope I'm there to see it happen."

With that, he left and I asked the waiter to bring me a new tablecloth, which he quickly did. Since the man left, there was no crime to report, and since I was in Chicago, I knew "nobody saw nuttin'."

So I finished my meal with the eyes of the people who had witnessed everything still on me until I left. It was pretty funny, as I never saw another person get up even to go to the restroom while I was there. Most people would say they were too afraid to get up, but this was Chicago, and I would argue that no one got up because they were all waiting to see if something else exciting was going to happen.

CHAPTER 8

Seeing the Obvious

While driving from our home in California en route to visit our cousins in Colorado, my family would often drive straight through without stopping because of the boring nature of the drive and because my father suffered from some kind of competitive pride disorder. We always raced through the back roads without stopping, just so my father could tell everyone how little time the drive took. I often heard him telling people that we had left the starting location later than we did just so it would sound like we made it to where we were going in less time. If you ever broke down the time it took us to get somewhere according to his time table, we would have had to have been traveling 130 miles per hour for ten straight hours. Also, there wouldn't have been time for any food stops, and we would have been peeing out the window. There we'd go, flying down the road at 130 miles per hour in our Pontiac station wagon with two boys, one on each side, peeing out the windows. Life doesn't get any better than that. To this day, I still have trouble urinating unless I'm traveling over 100 miles per hour in a car.

Delays drove my dad nuts, so during any rare stops, I of course dallied around just to see how long it took to cause him to snap. My brother and I would place bets as to how much time it would take. My brother was a good predictor, and he won most of these bets by getting the closest time. I don't think my brother ever cared about the bets; he just enjoyed watching my father go off on me when I spent too much time screwing around. I think my brother had a side bet with my mother as to how long I could go before my father clobbered me. The record stands today at six minutes flat, incidentally, the same amount of time it takes to fill a station wagon with gas.

My dad would load up the car with the exact supplies that would keep us fed during the twenty-four-hour drive in hopes of never stopping along the way. Thank God for mothers and gas stations, for without them, most kids would die on trips headed up by their fathers. My dad was an expert on the principles of "discommunication" (the dictionary defines *discommunication* as a verb meaning the act of ignoring all voice frequencies transmitted by kids or spouses during long drives). My dad could ignore bombs going off next to the car if it meant having to stop. He was the most focused human being I have ever known. My generation created the term ADD (attention deficit disorder) for those who needed to be medicated to eliminate life's distractions. My father probably needed to be medicated for FD (focus disorder). My brother, mother, and I generally needed some kind of medication to survive these long trips with my father.

My mother was the exact opposite of my father and was an expert at discommunication frequency interruption. She would pierce through my father's focus disorders with the precision of a skilled surgeon. She would adjust her communication frequency levels until she zeroed in on my father's, and once the right frequency was met, it was just a matter of time before we would be pulling off somewhere to stretch, eat, or pee. My mother's abilities to adjust her frequencies were incredible. First her tone and pitch would start off sounding exactly like a woman's voice, and to make the initial frequency sound normal, she would add a caring question or comment like, "I think we need to stop and stretch our legs, and if you see a place to stop, let's get a snack for the kids." It all sounded very cheerful to my brother and me, but my father never heard a word she said, and we would buzz right along the road passing any establishments that would have satisfied my mother's request.

While traveling though the western desert, you soon recognize when you pass an opportunity, the next one might not present itself for another hundred miles.

With my father's obvious inability to hear my mother's current frequency levels, she would change them to a deeper octave until her voice was so low that it matched those of the Tibetan monks who communicated using very low throat gurgles. Once my mother started her frequency interrogation process, my brother and I would sit back and wait, as we knew it was just a matter of time before we'd be running around in some roadside restaurant or souvenir stand parking lot being yelled at by my dad for playing tackle or our favorite game of smear-the-queer in the aisles of the store.

My mother had this process perfected to a point where if my father still couldn't hear her, she would summon the devil to speak for her. I swear, my brother and I both witnessed my mom's head rotating 360 degrees as she told my father in her deep demonic voice, "Pull the car over at the next opportunity or the authorities will be sifting through your dental records in order to identify the remains."

My father would grumble back, "We don't have time for stops."

Mom wouldn't miss a beat and would start digging through her purse, presumably looking for a weapon. We never knew what was in her purse, or as most would call it, her duffle bag. My dad, my brother, and I all thought her duffle bag purse was big enough to hold weapons. When any of us made her angry, she always started rifling through the bag. We never saw her actually remove any weapons, but we knew she had them, so when my dad wasn't listening, Mom would pull out the bag, and with that, we would usually stop.

Mothers and their children all suffer from small-bladder syndrome, while fathers, on the other hand, as has been noted from the many studies now chronicled by the *American Journal of Health*, do not have bladders at all. They have an empty open chest cavity located where you would usually find a heart. This cavity holds urine on long car trips. The different bladder sizes that men, women, and children have are further evidence that God has an incredible sense of humor.

My dad was an educated man, so on one of our trips when I was too young to remember, I guess I educated him about not listening to the family about pulling off for bathroom breaks. He wouldn't stop, and I couldn't hold it any longer, so I stood up in our car and soaked his luggage. You would have thought from that point on, he would never question the need to stop again, but being a retired military man, he simply threw an empty five-gallon paint bucket into the car for the long drives. It was funny though, if the car needed gas or if my dad needed to use the restroom, we'd stop without incident.

While en route to see the cousins on one of these trips, we were passing through Eli, Nevada, at the midnight hour. Eli is located in the Great Basin Desert, where you might see nothing larger than a bunny for what seemed like days. An occasional tumbleweed would go blowing around recklessly, or a shooting star might blaze a trail through the blackened sky along the world's loneliest highway. It was on one of these drives that my father was once again reminded of my odd sight abilities.

In the middle of the Nevadan desert, there are not many radio stations to choose from. Our radio had one of those late-night whack-job radio stations on talking about UFOs or two-headed monsters or something like that.

Everything was pretty dull in the car; only my father and I were awake. Suddenly, I yelled out, "Look out, Dad!"

My voice reverberated through the car. Shocked by my sudden outburst, my father, who had become sleepy during the nighttime drive in the middle of nowhere, swerved the car in terror.

72

Halfway through his skid, he started yelling at me uncontrollably, "What the hell are you shouting about? You're going to give me and everyone else in the car a damn heart attack!"

My father didn't stop because he saw an animal, but rather because my panicked yelling scared the hell out of him. My brother and mother were also stammering. Soon, they began shouting nonsense questions like, "What happened? Is everything okay? Did we hit something?"

Since there were no visible things on the road, my family went from peacefully enjoying the evening desert drive to seething in extreme anger in record time. The car we were all in went from a calm, quiet, serene atmosphere with harps playing in everyone's minds and angels dancing on the dashboard to a scene from Dante's *Inferno* all within a matter of a split second. I figured the family was going to beat me with sticks and leave my body in the desert for the coyotes to eat. They were that pissed. I tried to tell them what I was yelling about, but they were in no mood to listen. After all, there in the headlights, they could see nothing on the road. My family thought I had awakened from a bad dream, but that didn't lower the adrenaline that I had just caused to course my family's veins. Just as they were really laying into me, it happened. A large, male elk crossed the highway directly in front of our headlights less than ten feet from the front of the car. The bull elk was immediately followed by a herd of roughly two hundred other elk. If my father had not stopped, we would have collided with the herd of animals, which by best accounts, would be like driving through a herd of cattle on stilts.

Everyone in the car went from screaming at the nutty kid to instantaneous silence. My family's thoughts had gone from anger to astonishment.

He asked me in a surprised tone, "How did you see these animals? It's pitch-black out there?" He continued, "I don't get it; it's pitch-black out here. There is no way you could have seen them."

I was sitting in the front seat with my mother in the seat behind me, and once everything calmed down, she put her hands on my shoulders as though she was reassuring herself of her relationship with either something angelic or the devil itself.

My poor family, all still recovering from the earlier heart attack that I had given them with my middle-of-the-night screaming, was now suffering from shock. My brother was unable to utter a complete sentence for several weeks. I guess the shock was ultimately more than my mom could handle, because after returning home from the trip, she kept putting me in a box in front of the grocery stores with a sign on it saying, "Free kid." My dad responded differently from my mom and brother, as he began calling circus shows in hopes of leasing me out to make a couple of extra dollars.

One thing that couldn't be argued was the fact that my family had avoided an unseen event that was right in front of them, which would have caused a family tragedy. This was not an isolated event, as I used to pass along this type of information to my parents day and night as we drove along the country's highways and back roads all my life. I wasn't spotting herds of elk; instead, I would generally make them aware of deer, raccoons, skunks, etc. My family went from taking my observations as general mumblings of a kid and not really paying too much attention to them to listening to me like a congregation would concentrate on every word of the preacher. That night driving through the desert had changed everything, and I would never again be allowed to ride in the backseat; they would always have me up front.

Over the years, my ability to spot things improved. I often saw things others could not see. Whenever any neighbors lost their pets, young children, wallets, car keys, or whatever, they would always ask for my assistance to help locate their missing things. We were living in a rural area, so their pets and children never strayed too far away and finding them was generally an easy task, but the car keys and wallets were always a challenge. I never have figured out why people think you are able to locate wallets and keys if you are able to see auras.

My parents really never knew how to handle my abilities because of their own pride and because they didn't want the world to think their son was strange. As a result, they never really discussed my differences with too many people, especially strangers from out of town. My father's response at first was excitement, and at different times during his life, he would attempt to use my abilities for personal gain, but not in a bad way. My dad was simply trying to deal with my differences on his terms, and I believe he was always torn by the question, "Should I share my son's abilities with the world or not?"

My father never sorted things out completely, and his response to anyone who asked him about me was to chuckle quietly and pass it off as if the stories people would ask him about were simply the results of a prank or a joke. He went through life embarrassed by the attention that was focused on him regarding such events. He really never came to terms with my abilities, and even though my visual differences had saved his life on multiple occasions, he struggled with how to explain everything to others.

Much later in life, after I got married, I watched my wife face the same challenges. My wife's handling of the situation has always been exactly opposite of my father's. My wife is a very inquisitive person, who loves science and looks for oddities and questions in life that need to be answered. She is a very well-read person with the simple desire to not only find the answers to life's mysteries but also to present them to others in the hope that they can change the world for the better. After we were married, she soon realized that something was very different with my sight, as I would often tell her to look at one animal or another in the distance as we drove down the road. She would usually tell me that she didn't see anything at first but would finally spot what I was seeing with some additional focus. She would often get frustrated when I would tell her to look in one direction or another to see an animal when it was dark.

She would blurt out, "What are you pointing at? I don't see anything!"

I would tell her, "Look right there. Don't you see the deer?" I have always had the habit of reporting what I am seeing to those around me irrespective of whether it is daytime or nighttime.

Frustrated at my pushing the point and thinking I was trying to make her feel slighted for not seeing the animals, she would snap back, "No, I don't see anything." Then the animal would appear in the headlights. She really started to understand what was going on when I would tell her to slow down as animals were getting ready to cross the road in front of us in the middle of the night. She wouldn't see a thing, and all of a sudden, there the animal would be directly in our path with her headlights on it. Over time, she stopped questioning what I was seeing and started to analyze how I was able to see these things.

Over the years, my wife has heard many stories about my visual differences from my friends and family and even complete strangers. There were also many other events besides my being able to see animals at night that drove my wife's curiosity. For example, one afternoon, while coming back from a hike on the edge of town, I had noticed a camouflaged make-shift homeless camp hidden off in a remote part of the trail. I pointed the camp out to my wife; however, she was not able to see it. I wanted to go into this camp and roust the squatters out of the area, but my wife felt it was too dangerous to go it alone, so as a good husband, I listened to my wife's every word.

The following day, I had to leave our house early in the morning to catch a plane for an out-of-town meeting. Whenever I travel, my wife saves the local newspapers for me to read upon my return, so I can stay up on all of the current events. After I returned a couple of days later, I was reading the papers, and I noticed that witnesses swore they had heard what they thought were a woman's screams, but at the time, they were only able to locate an injured homeless man. There was quite a stir in town as many reports of a woman screaming kept coming in from the location where they found the injured homeless man, but he wasn't able to speak and no woman was located. Since only the man had been located after an extensive search, which had included a search-and-rescue helicopter, it was assumed that he was the only victim. The man had been brought into the hospital unconscious and unable to talk for a few days, and the other individuals had been rounded up from the hideaway, so everyone believed there had only been the one victim.

What was interesting to me was two days after I spotted the encampment, a group of homeless squatters residing in the camp caused a disturbance resulting from a fight that broke out late one evening. People heard screaming and yelling and an upset woman's voice. Local police, aided by forty-plus search-and-rescue members and a well-known psychic, converged upon the area to find where the voices had come from. After scouring the area for a day and a half, the rescue team found nothing. Believing that the screams also included those of a child, the desperate rescue team brought in the helicopter with heat-seeking capabilities to help locate whoever it was that had been screaming, which ultimately led to the hidden homeless camp.

The helicopter was able to locate a homeless man who had been injured in a fight with one of the other homeless men while trying to protect his wife and child. The man who was found was unconscious and taken to the local hospital to recover. As he recovered from his head injuries, he kept murmuring a child's name. After further investigation authorities finally located the women that had been screaming as she was being held against her will by the other homeless men, but no child had been located yet.

What was really interesting to my wife was that I had spotted the camp as a simple observation, yet it took a team of forty or more trained professionals, a psychic, and a helicopter with heat-seeking capabilities to locate the individuals.

After returning home from my trip and reading about the events that had taken place in town earlier in the week, I decided to take a look around the area, which was not too far from my house. What I found was a young girl balled up in a tree husk halfway up the trunk trying to stay hidden from passersby. She had been trained to live off the land by her parents, and she had been hiding there, simply waiting for them to return and pick her up.

Blur

After the child was reunited with her father and mother, the town went crazy trying to make sense out of the events that had taken place. The more I assisted in finding people, pets, and things, the more my friends and family accepted my freaky differences and stopped worrying about whether or not I posed some kind of threat to them.

CHAPTER 9

Troubled Teen Years and Pranks

The teenage years tend to be confusing for normal kids. When you add an oddity into the mix along with some cleverness, the confusion goes off the charts. Teenagers sometimes don't know their limits and can get caught up in the moment no matter how wild those moments become. Junior high and high school kids are also introduced to new elements like money, and all of the toys a young kid could wish for if he had enough of that money.

The same visual abilities to read people's personalities and feelings combined with my overzealous enjoyment of pranks, a high school kid's quest for extra money, and a touch of cleverness, got me and my closest friends into plenty of trouble many times during my youth.

Because of my ability to see and understand my targeted audiences through their energy levels, I quickly learned how far I could push the envelope without getting into serious trouble. Between the ages of ten and sixteen, I became bored with most of the things that teenagers get involved in and started developing my unusual talents in an unusual way.

When I was in junior high school, I used to do everything possible to antagonize the school principal and vice principal. Everything the principal and vice principal told the kids not to do, you could bet I would do.

The junior high school I attended was in a somewhat wealthy township, and the school kids had developed a small gambling problem, which the principal had to deal with. Kids were told they'd be hauled off in shackles to a dark room somewhere under the school where they would be severely beaten if they got caught gambling. We knew this threat was probably somewhat not true, but just to be sure, we purposely set up a couple of the slower kids to be caught just to see what would really happen. As these kids were captured, you could hear their final shrieks as they were dragged to the secret room to face their punishment. These kids would usually show up again in a week or two, but their personalities would be somewhat subdued as they were reintroduced into the general population, no doubt as a direct result of the severe beatings they had taken while in solitary confinement.

You can learn a lot from watching what the process and the punishment are when others get taken down by the man. The school's process was simple; the teachers would merely wait a few minutes for recess to start and then just open their classroom doors and grab anyone they saw pitching coins outside their doors. It was like catching fish with a net for them.

It's important here to point out how easy it was initially for these teachers to catch kids gambling. At the highpoint of our illicit activities, if you walked through the school during recess, fire escape breaks, or lunch, you could easily find behind every wall or in any back hall, many of the students pitching coins at the walls to see who could get closest. The coins tossed were not the prize; they were merely the tokens used to settle the bets. Most coin-tossing bets were for one or five dollars, but a toss for twenty dollars was not rare. If you were the fortunate winner, you could make a good childhood income. As the greed factor grew and the gambling bug blossomed with these kids, more and more of them started playing the game and more and more of them were being hauled off to the secret room to take their punishment.

Knowing how easy it was for the teachers to catch the kids, we had to come up with a way to deter these teachers from opening their doors. The solution was actually easy, and once operation "Keep the Door Shut" was enacted, the teachers would never again involve themselves in our affairs.

The most effective clandestine counterintelligence operations involve the use of everyday people and common objects. To prove this point, I had all of the kids show up a little early one day with bags of dog droppings if they had dogs. They were then instructed to empty the joyful bags of stink into the trash cans that were conveniently placed outside every classroom door. The kids were then told to partially fill these cans with water. At the first recess, the kids went into the halls as they always did, but once the last kids exited each room, they closed the doors and everyone rushed to lean the trash cans loaded with water and doggy delights against the doors. A few minutes later, the teachers opened their doors at roughly the same time thinking they would be plucking young gamblers from the halls. The kids heard hysterical screams instead. They could tell exactly which teachers had opened their doors by the locations of the screaming. It was like an orchestra from hell as the initial screaming was replaced with a plethora of cursing, as the teachers were now basking in their new delightful perfume. Instead of the teachers reaching out and grabbing their handful of daily gamblers, they received a wet, smelly lesson, which introduced for the first time in history the idea that maybe kids aren't as dumb as many teachers believe them to be.

I was a hero at my school for crafting the idea, as the kids all got a couple of days off since the school had to be closed in order for them to clean the awful smell out of the classes. All of the dog owners were also happy because for the first time, their kids had picked up as many doggy droppings in the neighborhood as they could find in preparation for operation "Keep the Door Shut," leaving parents perplexed as to why. I'm sure the parents found out later why all of the kids had worked so hard once they heard the news from the school.

From that time on, since teachers were no longer regulating these activities because of fear of reprisal from the inmates, it became tough to walk through the halls and the back alleys of our school without seeing some of the kids tossing their coins in hopes of cleaning the other kids out. I took to perfecting my skills of pitching coins like a preacher takes to the Bible or a drunk takes to booze.

As with all things where overstimulation exists, people eventually became bored and looked for other excitement. After a while, there were only a couple of us who were consistently winning the tosses, so the prizes were dwindling, and we too lost interest. The coin-tossing games simply died a natural death, but new games and new ways of getting all of your school chums' dough were merely waiting to be established for this eager audience.

The other form of gambling that replaced the pitching game was a game called "odd man out." This game consisted of three players who would shake a single coin in their hand and all three would show their coins simultaneously. If I had a heads showing (the face of a coin) and the others both showed tails (the reverse side of the coin), then I was the odd man out, and they would give me whatever amount of money the bet was for. Similarly, if I showed a tail and they both showed a face, then I was the odd man out and would be paid. I quickly learned that if I teamed up with one of the other two children prior to the gaming events and they always ended up with the opposite side of the coin that I had, one of us would win every bet, guaranteed. My friends and I started cleaning up on the playground. Kids would bring in all of their allowances each week to try to win. Of course parents were not thrilled with little Tommy or Suzy coming home broke each week.

A school investigation was launched, and the perpetrators were named over and over. Before the school could wipe out the small-time crime wave that I was instrumental in starting, they had to catch us in the act.

Suspension and expulsion was the threat of the day. After initial threats passed ineffectively, the school administrators started to get crafty. The school hired undercover law enforcement aided by some of the school-children who had changed teams against the students to entrap the primary gambling ring. These children who teamed up with the police were primarily students who had lost large sums of money in previous weeks and wanted justice served.

You would have thought that I was peddling booze or women during the Prohibition by the sheer numbers of undercover police and turncoat students that plagued our sacred school grounds. For a couple of weeks, it was difficult to find a place to play our gambling games. Kids with gambling weaknesses could be seen throughout the grounds flopping around and talking to themselves while they went through their withdrawals. Kids who had lost their bikes, toys, family televisions, coats, backpacks, and other small appliances were now being escorted to and from class. The lawless society, which I had a hand in initially creating, now had a new look and feel, and the lawlessness was now definitely over. I felt like Doc Holliday and Wyatt Earp were now in town looking to shoot me down.

It wasn't all bad though, because since many kids kept losing their lunch money and couldn't afford their normal daily rations, they began to lose a lot of weight. During the gambling heyday, our school won awards for having the fittest student population in the country. The gym teacher received undue praise, and a huge banner was hung in front of the school.

Even though the school was basking in their new recognitions associated having all of the skinny kids, they knew they still had to deal with the dark evil that lurked under its surface, and the school continued to pay youthful-looking adults to meld into the school's population with hopes of catching the perpetrators. Schools always overreact, and kids never understand their actions fully. I thought the school should have added bright neon lights like they have in Vegas to increase tourism and spending at the campus. We could have added more and more games to increase the house's earnings. It would have been great, and our school would have had more money than all the others. That couldn't be bad, could it?

School officials had different thoughts though, and all of their new-found law introduced itself and started sending some of the children home. In spite of everyone else's fear of imminent capture, I knew I would be all right, as I knew whom to avoid simply as a result of my ability to see who had tight energy levels as a result of their deception, so I kept on gambling and winning without getting caught. The principal and vice principal, knowing that I was the kingpin, were so upset with the fact that I couldn't be caught that they took a different and more direct approach. First, they called me into the office and told me they knew of my level of involvement and that all of the other children who were now working for them and the police had ratted me out. They told me I would be immediately expelled if caught and that capture was imminent. I asked what would happen beyond expulsion and was told all my money would be confiscated and used to buy trees and benches for the school. My parents were also immediately contacted and informed of the severity and the dire situation at school. My parents also threatened me with public floggings and ultimate prison time. They weren't as concerned with the events at school as they were with the possibility of my being home more after expulsion, which in their minds was just around the corner.

My brother was cool with everything and started selling tickets around town for people to take tours of the home that housed the next Al Capone. My brother always enjoyed the position that I left him in, that of the guy who did nothing wrong in life, but was famous for having a brother who always managed to walk on the third rail without getting shocked.

I, on the other hand, took these threats all very seriously. I knew if captured, I would be making big rocks into small ones. I also knew I preferred home-cooked meals to the possibility of using a prison shank to get what I wanted from other inmates. So I thought about my options very carefully and decided to be cautious with my gaming operations. I would from then on only gamble with those children who had not been completely corrupted by the adults. I didn't care if they told on me, because I knew I would have to be caught in the act.

What the school officials, police, and other students didn't know was that I could identify who was being honest with me and who was not because of my ability to see energy levels. At that time, I still thought every person alive could see exactly what I could see from the energy levels. Looking back at this ability, and as mentioned earlier, I remember being very confused watching boys and girls traverse their sexuality during their teenage years, but this ability to see energy levels sure helped me read people when it came to gambling.

When playing these children for money, I could tell instantly when one of the rogue spy children was setting kids up for capture because of their very thin levels of energy. The more nervous someone would get, the thinner their energy levels became. The more comfortable a person was, the thicker this energy wave became. When I saw these thin levels, I wouldn't get involved in the gaming, and sure enough, after a few short minutes, in came the police and hauled people away, every time. After a couple of weeks of picking which events I would participate in, I found the school administration was becoming more and more irritated with me and my ability to elude capture even though I was always right in front of their eyes. The school was also getting very tired of sending home so many other children each week without me in the mix. I was again brought directly before the principal and vice principal and was again threatened with public decapitation and of ultimately having my remains fed to goats. I asked them if I could make a donation to the school fund and buy trees, benches, and a bronze water sculpture in the likeness of both men for the school. My parents raised me properly, so I felt compelled to share 5 to 10 percent of my winnings with the organization that helped create my current occupation. They seemed to think about the idea for a split second, but soon dismissed it as probably being a bad idea.

During this discussion, the nurse even visited and checked the back of my neck and my head for the numbers 666.

For the next two weeks, the situation continued followed by a trip to the principal's office on Friday afternoon. This time, the principal informed me that since I had done such a good job eluding everyone that they we going to reward me by dropping all accusations against me and that starting Monday morning, I would have a clean slate to work from and bygones would be bygones.

The problem was that while talking to me, both the principal and vice principal had little to no energy levels showing, a state of being that I only see when someone is dying or dead. Since I knew both men to be very healthy and guessing that I couldn't be as lucky as to have them both die over the weekend, I decided their story of letting bygones be bygones to be a well-thought-out lie. They had something serious in mind for me Monday morning. When I finally left their office, I felt like a baby seal jumping into a tank of killer whales. What I knew for sure was I would not be coming to school on Monday. I went directly to my locker and took home everything with the exception of three textbooks that I had and headed home.

Monday morning rolled around, and I had caught a terrible cold over the weekend. As I lay deathly ill, knowing the end was coming—I could really turn on the sympathy switch when necessary—my mother came into my room around noon to inform me that most of my closest friends had been carted off to juvenile hall or sent home having been caught up in a surprise gambling sting operation, which had taken place at school that morning. My mother also informed me that the school had called her to check my flu symptoms very carefully to ensure validity. The principal was very direct with my mother and said I was the number-one reason for the police ambush, and they couldn't for the life of them understand how circumstances led to my being out of school that day.

After that, I figured I had caused enough chaos for the school, the administration, local law enforcement, and my fellow students and decided to hang up my illicit activities for good, which I did.

To celebrate my retirement, I decided one last prank was in order to seal the day. Knowing that the principal always used the restroom each morning, I decided to place a couple of ketchup packs that I had brought to school that morning under the toilet seat. As the principal sat down on the seat during his daily visit, the packs, pressed by his weight on the seat, popped and shot ketchup all over his suit. I laughed very hard to myself as he walked past me with his backside covered in red. I would soon finish junior high school and move on to high school. I would miss my days there, but I know from direct remarks made to me by the faculty that they were not going to miss me at all.

After I graduated from junior high school, I prepared for my move up to high school. My transition was the same as every other child's: getting a summer job to earn some money, going on dates with the local girls, playing baseball, and picking a fight with one hundred plus members from the local motorcycle gang. Okay, I lied; I didn't really have many dates at that age. During the school year, my parents felt sports would be too much for my schedule and instead opted to keep me occupied with chores around our ranch. I can't much blame them for wanting to keep me busy at the ranch, because there were more than enough animals to care for, and it was their hope that this business would also keep me from devising my next crime wave at school. They were correct.

While working at the ranch, I would always dream of playing professional baseball. I set up a target to mirror a baseball catcher's mitt position, as it would be at home plate. I walked off the necessary 60.6 feet of distance between the pitching mound rubber to the batter's box and threw rocks for hours until nightfall. With all of this practice, my targeting and delivery became very good. I could hit most moving or stationary targets. I even developed the talent for knocking squirrels off phone lines, birds off branches, and biker gang members out of lounge chairs while seated in their club yard chairs.

The biker club house that was located near our ranch was an oddity to say the least. The house they hung out in had been built in the 1930s and had become completely run down over the years. A quarter of all of the windows were broken; the roof had holes in it; and a painter would have trouble painting it because most of the wood was rotten beyond repair. Yet it seemed to attract a couple hundred people to it every Saturday evening. The point of interest to me and my friends was the fact that multimillion-dollar ranches, which were built many years later, surrounded the biker hangout. All of the families despised the inhabitants of the biker hangout, but no one ever dared say anything to them for fear of reprisals. All of the ranch owners would simply look away from the hangout as they drove past, because direct eye contact would turn them into stone much faster than peering into Medusa's eyes. In fact, one of our neighbors had witnessed one of the other neighbor's demise when his dog got loose in the bikers' yard. The man caught his dog, picked it up, and came face-to-face with a biker when he stood up with the dog. Rumor was the man's stone carcass was mounted over in the entryway and the bikers cooked and ate the dog.

With all of the bad press constantly circulating around the bikers and the hangout, I felt it was my duty to run them out of town. I envisioned the local neighborhood celebrating my great feat by throwing the town a party, along with putting together a parade with at least three or four floats and a band, changing the town name to my name, and retiring the date from the calendar as a sacred national holiday, or at least a state holiday. My enthusiasm grew, so I invited my closest friends to join me on my quest.

Many of the ranches in the area had egg-laying chickens. If you've ever been around chickens, you know that the average family has to eat roughly forty-three eggs daily to keep ahead of the egg production. If the families get behind the egg count and don't keep consumption at peak usage, then they will either end up owning four hundred new chickens each year from the hatchings or they end up throwing away a lot of uneaten eggs. You simply can't give away enough eggs when your neighbors all have chickens, so they don't want your eggs either.

My strategy included collecting eggs over the next several weeks and leaving them in the sun to "ripen" in preparation for the upcoming Annual Rock Band Fest at the local biker hangout. A slightly steep hill was perched roughly one hundred yards from the side of the hangout. The side of the hill was completely covered with the healthiest patch of the sharpest, nastiest, most infectious, and tallest thistle weeds known to man. The needle points on these thistles were six inches long on the smallest plants and twelve inches long on the big plants. One of my friends swore a man would traverse the hill weekly and hand sharpen every thistle. If you were unlucky enough to get within the reach of one of the thistles and were scraped or poked by one of the needle points, you would immediately swell up and start scratching at your skin madly. Timmy Jenkins, who lived down the street from the thistles with his elderly grandparents, once lost a ball in the thistles. When he tried to retrieve it, he met with several of the needles and instantly swelled up to four times his normal size to the point where all of his clothes burst off with the exception of his underwear briefs. His underwear briefs being left on made things much worse for Timmy, because with his swollen body, he actually looked like a sumo wrestler who had gotten lost in the neighborhood. Timmy's elderly grandfather suffered from poor eyesight and simply thought Timmy was a bear that was after his animals. He shot several rounds of buckshot into Timmy's behind before realizing it was him. That was the last time any of us have ever heard of anyone getting close to these frightful plants.

The thistles were so dense that no animals would ever chance walking through them. The hill was just steep enough to keep the rancher who owned it from ever plowing it under, so this plot of land had never been changed by man. Topography maps have proven that this piece of land exists today the same way it had during the time of the dinosaurs, and there was quite a bit of speculation that this single plot of land may have in fact been responsible for the demise of the dinosaurs.

The annual get-together was the bikers' largest each year, attracting several hundred bikers, a dozen bands, eight hundred thousand gallons of

Budweiser, four hundred and fifty pounds of marijuana, one thousand bags of Doritos, three thousand condoms, and one bar of soap in the bathroom. We never figured out what they did with the soap.

My plan was a simple one. Over the next few weeks, I would walk in through the thistle maze during the day so I could see and avoid the thorny plants and drop off a hundred or so sun-ripened eggs into a small open space dead in the middle of the thistle patch. This open space was approximately twelve feet by twelve feet and would allow me and my cohorts in crime the necessary space needed for throwing the weapons of mass destruction. The challenge for my friends and I would be getting ourselves into position under the cover of darkness on the night of the attack. Over the next couple of weeks, we loaded up the piles of eggs and attempted many evening practice runs into the thistles, losing one or two soldiers in each mock attempt.

Finally, the date of infamy was upon us. That evening, we could hear the bikes rolling up the street seemingly for hours and the bands blaring away. The bands actually sounded pretty good, so in some respect, it was a shame what was about to happen. Darkness overtook our position, and the only visible lights were those from the party. I stood, took aim, and threw the eggs as far as I could. The eggs would disappear into the darkness and would reemerge for a split second into the lights of the clubhouse exploding onto the partygoers. You could hear the screams and yells of those receiving direct hits from the eggs. After unloading half of the eggs onto the unsuspecting crowd, we retreated to the ground. The bands stopped playing. The crowd was going crazy throwing out colorful and descriptive threats, and everyone was milling around in circles like ants in an anthill. We sat quietly as the crowd widened beyond its original boundaries. Just when everything started to get back to normal, I stood up and resumed launching the remaining eggs.

Once again, the crowd came apart at its seams, yelling threats, saying they were going to do impossible acts to us and our families when they caught us. Many started to evacuate the party while others went in search of the unknown assailants. Many of the now-victimized partygoers intuitively guessed we were somehow located in the thistles but dared not enter. Those who did try to enter were immediately turned back by the painful greeting program of the thistle jungle. We had to keep from laughing as we heard their anguish.

"Son of a bitch!"

"Damn it, these things are sharp!"

"Ow, damn it!"

Just to make sure no one entered our hideout, we added quite a few cow patties to the entrance area of the thistle garden. If you didn't see the patties and didn't know to jump over them, you would definitely proceed no further. Again, their remarks continued to fly.

"What the hell is that smell?"

"I'm not going in there."

My friends and I lay perfectly still to avoid giving away our location. Since the party had drifted toward us in the darkness, my friends were quite nervous that we were going to be dead very soon. Situations never really bothered me too much, as I could see people from the auras very well at night and I knew we were fine. After a while, the bikers grew tired of getting poked by the thistles and stepping in cow pies while trying to find us, and they eventually left.

CHAPTER 10

Sometimes Good People Die

I hadn't heard anything from my buddy in the service since our last encounter in Chicago several months earlier. One morning, while I was traveling in Seattle, he approached me in a small café in the waterfront district with instructions to join his team for a discussion they were having with a dissident that they had picked up trying to enter the US illegally at the US and Canadian border.

The man in question was Syrian-born and was being less than cooperative; in fact, he was being completely unresponsive to questions posed to him by US authorities, and I was asked to help out with the process, which I agreed to do.

As we talked at the café prior to meeting with the man in question, I laughed to myself. I had glanced at his hand and noticed the now-healed scars where my fork had left a permanent message from our last, less amicable meeting. He noticed my expression and commented how he was enjoying this meeting much more than the last.

We finished our breakfast and climbed into a car that his team had waiting for us to take us to the meeting that awaited our presence. No one spoke until we reached our destination: an old house on the outskirts of the city. Before leaving the car, we reviewed some classified documents outlining the past of the man who was being interrogated. He had very suspect past associations with some questionable people and was obviously involved in some very shady dealings. There was no question that this was a real player intent on damaging US relationships internationally and more harm would come to US interests if we were unsuccessful at getting the truth out of him.

Prior to the questioning, the team told me what to expect from the US interrogation processes. They told me not to be alarmed, but simply watch the proceedings and tell them through my reviews of his aura when it was known to me that he was lying.

Once we finished our preliminary discussions, we climbed out of the car and headed up the front walkway of the old house to meet the man in question. Suddenly, out of nowhere, shots rang out from all directions and the men I had just driven to the house with were all falling into pools of their own blood. They fought back gallantly against their foes, who overpowered them in both number and firepower. How I was missed has haunted me to this day, and I can only assume the assailants were instructed not to shoot me as any one of them could have easily ended my life at that moment. Just as quickly as the incident started, it ended with the aggressors immediately fleeing in their vehicles.

There I was standing on a porch in the middle of an old neighborhood surrounded by three dead men, who moments before, had been full of life. My ears were still ringing from the barrage of gunfire that had taken place only seconds before. As I looked down at my fallen comrades lying in their own blood, I was grabbed by the inhabitants from inside the house and was immediately escorted out through the back into a waiting van. I was returned to my hotel.

I was told only one thing by the man in charge, "This never happened, so pull yourself together and compose yourself."

My thoughts kept circling back to the US intelligence service man whom I had dealt with many times over the years, and I wondered what his family would be told. Did he even have a family? Would there be any record of what just happened? I felt bad for the guy and his team. I thought about how much I had hated them in the past for the troubles they had caused me and my family, but now I realized the importance of what they provided for the security of our nation and the personal risks they faced every day while just doing their jobs. For the first time in many years, I felt lost and confused; the guy who had created so much chaos in my life was dead, and I wondered if his and his team's absence would open the door to others in the international sector to get to me. I couldn't help but wonder; *Did this guy and his team harass me through the years and at the same time provide me and my family unknown protection? What will happen now that they have been eliminated?* I immediately missed them, and at the same time, I now understood how much admiration I had for them. I only wished I had known then what I knew now so I could have told them.

Later that evening while watching the news, I learned how things get covered up when the government doesn't want people to know about them. It was reported that gang violence had erupted in the neighborhood, but everything was now under control and the gang members had all been arrested. I was never interviewed, and to this date, all I can tell you is, "Nothing ever happened!"

CHAPTER 11

Marriage and Discovery
of a Difference

My wife and I grew up thousands of miles apart, she a Southern Belle and me a Northern Yankee. She was raised on a farm in the Kentucky countryside; I was raised in a Northern California suburb. She was trained by her mother in the traditional Southern style how a Southern lady should act, talk, and properly present herself and how to entertain. I was trained by the neighborhood kids and their families. I don't want to give the wrong impression here; I didn't grow up in the hood or in the projects, and my family never needed or wanted for anything, but when you grow up in a city or the suburbs, you are raised and shaped by the community you live in, good or bad. When you live in the country, you are raised by a much smaller community, usually your immediate family, church, and school. The standards that are acceptable in the Southern traditions are not the same standards Northerners live by in the city.

Standard entertainment in the South is anything but typical. Entertainment almost always includes engaging in a wonderful meal with the main focus not being the meal at all but rather the conversation that follows. It matters not how delightful or how lavish these Southern-style meals are, because the meals themselves are for substance only, a kind of "since we're gonna talk, we may as well have some treats too" situation. If you have never experienced a Southern-style meal before, "y'all" must.

For every Southern meal—breakfast, lunch, dinner, snacks, and after dinner—treats are always creative, tasty, and involve a tradition of conversation with either family or friends or both. A typical breakfast would include grits, homemade biscuits, and thick slabs of ham prepared in the Southern tradition of hanging and salt curing the pig over time to ensure the meat is perfect, as though the good Lord prepared it himself. Eggs are always included, but it's my belief that Southerners include eggs for color or decoration to every breakfast because they cannot possibly add anything to an already tasty meal.

Although it is the next obvious meal if you are used to eating three meals each day, lunch to the Southerner is merely another opportunity for crafted dialogue. I'll ferret to guess that if you ask people from the South what they ate for lunch, they will fail to answer correctly every time. If you ask them who they shared lunch with and what topics were discussed, they will talk for hours. This is because the Southern people have, in my observation, developed the best skills of anyone in the world around proper, interesting, and warm communication. These skills are shared by family and friends during every lunch hour. I'm always enjoyably astonished by the talent of a Southerner to express absolutely anything better than anyone else in the world.

A simple example of this would be people other than Southerners discussing a topic, say recounting a new car that had been purchased. Non-Southerners would tell you they bought a car, and they would tell you the type and color of the car, whether or not they liked it; they may also tell you the price they paid for the car…and that's it, story over.

Not so fast for the Southerners. They would report to you every aspect about the car, where it was made, why it was created, the chronicles and historical significance of the people who created the car, the history of the automobile industry, how eleven of their friends owned the same car, how much research they did preceding the purchase of the car, why the price they paid for the car was the best price ever, why the person they bought the car from was the finest person ever to work with in the car industry, and so on. Everything is personalized in a very decisive, competent manner.

After chatting with a Southerner about the car, you'd feel so confident and satisfied that you would rush out and acquire one for yourself, your teenager, the postman, and the neighbor's fifteen-year-old adolescent just to make sure that when the kid turns sixteen and can legally drive, he or she ends up in the greatest car ever. This is true for any conversation with any Southerner regarding something he or she bought and enjoyed. On the other side of the tale though, if a Southerner is sold something bad, no one else in the world will ever suffer the same misfortune because everyone will hear about the ghastly purchase.

The traditional Southern suppers are also much different than Northern dinners. I would compare a standard Southern supper to a formal Northern wedding, just replace the bride and groom with the neighbors from the next farm over. Suppers are long in the South with many courses served throughout the evening, similar to what you'd find in Europe. Conversations are inclusive, offering the opportunity for the participants to ask many well-thought-out questions, which other participants have to ponder and give witty answers to. Southern meals are no place for an amateur conversationalist. If you are not able to participate effectively, you will be forgotten by all and swept off to some distant field outside of Atlanta where Confederate taps and a final recital of the song, "Dixie," will be played as you are dismissed permanently to a back holler never to be heard from again.

If you are new to the South and are accidentally invited to a supper, it's also helpful if a friend is good with comedic flair to pull you out of difficult situations. Anyone who knows me is very aware that I have no off switch between what is on my mind and what comes out of my mouth. What I think is what you hear. Some people say this is great, because they can genuinely trust what I say.

My father-in-law has the ability to throw out funny lines and stories that always seem to mitigate many of my responses for the audience on hand. I am fairly certain that without his comedic capabilities, I would have been strung up and set ablaze creating a fire as big as when Sherman marched through Richmond.

The Northern-style dinners are quite different and generally more pragmatic in nature. Northerners eat because we know we have to or we will die. Things are faster-paced in the North; idle conversation around meals is nonexistent. In the North, people talk because they have to, not because they want to. If you think this is wrong, just try listening to how a Northerner sounds when he or she talks versus a Southerner. If you can tell me that a New Yorker's accent is as sexy or peaceful as that of a lady from the South, then I'll concede this point. Since you can't, I'll speak as a Northerner and simply say shut up with your wrong opinions. Northerners talk with one another, while they are doing something else—golfing, driving, jogging, etc. It is not common for a Northerner to have conversations last more than fifteen to twenty minutes during a meal. Any period longer than the allotted fifteen to twenty minutes causes Northerners great anxiety and discomfort. If you don't believe this, try this experiment the next time you go for a meal in a Southern state and try it again in a Northern state. In both locations, send the waiter or waitress away when he or she comes to your table to take your order, saying you need more time to make your decision on what you feel like eating. Sounds harmless enough, right? When you do this in the South, the waitperson will recognize you as an admirable person, highly skilled with the gift of good conversation, the beneficiary of a positive moral upbringing, and a doubtless a charm to be around. Low classical music will start playing through the restaurant's stereo system, and a light breeze will begin circulating through the enclosed diner as angels pass through overhead playing harps and dropping floral petals on you and any neighboring clientele.

Try this same strategy in a Northern state, say New York or Massachusetts, and see what happens. First, you will never see your server again unless he or she comes back to stick a butter knife through your hand. The servers respect no one who does not enter the restaurant ready to play ball. What you want to eat should be what you thought you wanted to eat before you entered the restaurant. Most Northerners do not read a menu because they know what they want to eat before walking through the door. In the North, you don't go into an Italian restaurant because you are going to ask if they have calzone or lasagna, you go to an Italian restaurant because you know they make that stuff there. If they don't have the calzone or lasagna on the menu because you're not in an Italian restaurant, you tell them to make it anyway. They will; it may suck, but they don't care, because it's your problem. The only reason they give you a menu in the North is because they know Northerners are not comfortable with conversations and they have to have something in their hands as a way to avoid any potentially direct eye contact that could ultimately lead to painful divulgence of innermost secrets. The absence of such a distraction has been proven to cause soul-searching discussions and anxiety-driven revelation of facts in the presence of others.

In fact, one evening when my wife and I were first dating, I had a friend join us for supper. She extended her Southern hospitality to my friend and proceeded to open the slow-paced Southern-style conversation. I could see my friend had no idea how to respond. He became confused and looked like he felt trapped. His face turned red, and he started sweating. He started talking in foreign tongues as though he had lost his mind. Not deterred at all, my wife kept to her Southern upbringing, calmly and methodically talking to my friend during the meal. My friend finally couldn't take the pressure any longer, fell to the floor, had a seizure, and imploded before our very eyes.

My wife and I learned early on during our relationship how differ-ent we were in the same ways that most couples do. When you are close to someone, these differences present themselves frequently. Sometimes, the differences are small and do not seem to be anything to worry about. Other differences may be much more important to the individuals, and some adjustment may be required by both parties to make the differences work for the good of the relationship.

Our differences presented themselves in the normal way and just came out over time. If you had asked me about our differences, I would have answered in the usual way of acknowledging my wife had some issues that probably needed to be corrected, like her lack of professional driving skills, not properly worshiping the ground I walked on, not properly peel-ing the grapes before serving them to me—you know, the normal stuff. One day out of the blue, my wife said, "We are going to a counselor to discuss some issues."

Now any guy will tell you the word *counselor* is simply a code word used in a relationship to inform you that you're a mess and you need to be mentally reprogrammed to meet your wife's basic standards of accept-ability. Being even one step below this standard allows for the husband to be publicly humiliated, scoffed at by the wife's friends, and quickly moved out into an apartment in the wee hours of the evening never to be seen again. I had seen this happen to some of my friends who had thought their partners were okay with them coming home after being fired for drinking on the job, having other women in relationships who had not been prop-erly introduced to their wives, or betting the rent money on the next sure thing. Since that was never my style, I thought my wife had mistakenly signed me up for counseling, but no mistake had been made.

She wouldn't discuss why she wanted to go to counseling, so I guessed she had some real issues to deal with probably related to the awful life that she had suffered at the hands of her brutally controlling family. But, wait, her family was normal, as that word was defined in the *Webster's Dictionary*. After checking her family off as being okay, I decided we must be going in to discuss ways to help her with her mean boss or overly nosey friends, but again, no issues and they were checked off the list as okay. Then it came to me; those damn neighbors were always a real problem. So I got my pad of paper out, made some notes about my nutty neighbors, hopped into the car with my wife, and headed off to counseling.

This was going to be a great meeting; we would finally straighten out those messed-up neighbors once and for all. This counselor would hold the box with the answers to all of life's questions. We would be spoon-fed the formula for success and answer all of our questions and open the doors to our deepest thoughts. We would rule the earth.

Once seated in the room, I was immediately amazed by all of the puzzles that had been left as piles of incomplete invitations to occupy the minutes of boredom of waiting for our appointment time. They had 3-D puzzles, Rubik's Cubes with colors not properly aligned, math puzzles left stranded on the waiting room table, all just begging to be solved and neatly stacked away. I hate messes left by others and cannot simply sit in a room while a mess stands in front of me, so the mess has to be remedied and stored away properly and respectfully.

Little did I know, this puzzle was part of a larger test and what was laid out in front of me needed to be solved. I was being judged on my puzzle-solving capabilities. I was unaware that I was being evaluated from the time I entered the waiting room. I was filmed and timed as a way to see how I viewed things such as these. My wife had been noticing that I would focus on certain activities that others would not even recognize. She knew something was different, but since she didn't see the world as I did, she really couldn't come to terms with some of the differences.

We learned that I saw different colors than most people, and while most people read by seeing the letters on a page, I read by seeing the white paper and noticing the letter outlines that were missing; we learned what a Kirlian camera was and how it, like me, could measure energy levels.

The lessons learned from this meeting demonstrated to me that even with the great differences between upbringing, communication, and

Northern and Southern traditions. My wife and I are proof that no matter how different you are with your partner and friend, and I need to stress the word, *"different,"* anything is possible. This also demonstrates how difficult it was when my wife first truly learned about my unusual visual differences.

CHAPTER 12

Haunted House on the Hill

It was early one morning, and I couldn't sleep. As much as I wanted to, I just tossed and turned and lay there wide awake. Everything that I had ever feared in my life flashed through my mind, from having to eat my mom's liver-and-onion dinners to achieving my somewhat large goals as well as other work things. The dumbest things seemed huge, and real concerns seemed insurmountable. I looked over at my wife, who knew my fears and worries, and watched as she comfortably slept away. Man, was I pissed. How could she let me deal with my worries alone? When you get married, isn't it "for better or for worse"? I was awake worrying about the "worse" of it while she was dreaming away, and it looked like she was getting the "better" of it.

Well, there I was wide awake with my mind traveling through space and time quicker than any formulas that I had ever studied in my old physics class back at the university predicted was possible. I had to get out of the house, walk around, and get a taste of some fresh air. I whispered quietly to my wife that I was going to walk downtown and wanted to know if she wanted to join me. She was unresponsive to my inquires; she lay there like a lump all snuggled away under the sheets. Man, did she ever look comfy! I couldn't wake her, as I would have felt too guilty taking her away from her blissful moment, so I slipped out of bed without a noise, got dressed, and stepped out the front door.

Our house is located in town, a Victorian period western town established during the gold-mining days. The town has survived and prospered through the years into a historical destination point that people travel to from all over the world. The town's old Victorian homes line the streets with rich history, some good and some not so good. If you are a history buff, you know that these old gold-mining towns saw all kinds of excitement throughout the years. Our town had several Old West–style high-noon duels, stagecoach robberies, hangings, card game shootouts, murders, and other such events. The town's residents included future presidents, senators, Supreme Court judges, saloon owners, prostitutes, miners, and robbers. People were making a killing off of the gold mines and that attracts both good and bad people and a whole lot of excitement.

As I headed out the front door, I decided I would just take a quick stroll through town to relieve a little tension. Upon my return home, all would be better. I was really excited to walk through town by myself on this quiet evening, as it reminded me of days past when I was a young kid and stayed out late for the first time. My anticipated walk made me feel excited and alive, as I envisioned seeing my little town from a different perspective. Instead of the usual crowds that flocked through the old picturesque gold-mining town looking for trinkets and souvenirs, I assumed the town would be locked up and quiet.

I walked into town expecting to feel more relaxed, but I started to feel a little odd, slightly lost, and somewhat confused. I had an unusual feeling, almost as though I was being watched. It was an eerie sensation, one you'd pass off as just one of those odd feelings that probably have more to do with the oddity of the moment than anything worth really wondering about.

Many people say our town is haunted and many people have claimed they have seen spirits at some of the old digs in town. We have even had professional ghost chasers film their television shows in town as they try to capture the elusive evidence and prove once and for all that ghosts truly exist. My thoughts on the subject matter have always been swayed by logic, which leads me to believe there's a sensible answer for the causes of people thinking they are in the presence of ghosts and spirits. I really have never believed that ghosts exist at all.

What has been hard to understand in my life is that I have seen these oddities because of their auras. I have never been able to explain this, but when we are in town and sometimes in my own home, I see these energy patterns as they move through a room, as though they are walking. My sightings are sometimes confirmed by our dog's hysterical barking and growls. I still believe there is some logical reason or a hidden explanation for why this happens, but I just haven't found the answers yet.

My wife and daughter get pretty upset when the dog becomes aggressive, as she is normally a very calm and peaceful pet. Very seldom does she ever get upset. I always see the energy pattern around her when she becomes aggressive, but I have never told my family what I'm seeing, so as not to upset them. Instead, my response has always been to act as though the dog is just a little goofy at times.

Have you ever thought you had seen a ghost or felt a ghostly presence? Many people go through life as I do, discounting most things that they can't see as nonexistent. People naturally have a need for factual, quantifiable proof of anything unknown or invisible to them. In a world as religious as the one we live in, people continuously fight wars, live with their conscious minds, pray to a god they have never met, take photos of things they see for proof of its existence, breathe the unseen air around them, understand the invisible aspects of gravity, but if you say you believe in ghosts, you're considered a nut job.

Have you ever witnessed a family dog attack an empty space as though an intruder with a weapon was in full attack on your family? The dog growls, snarls, and barks, fully showing all of its teeth and acting as it would if an intruder were truly present, and we chuckle at the odd behavior. What if there was a dangerous intruder present? Would we still be comfortably laughing at the situation, or would our demeanor be somewhat modified? You saw absolutely nothing, but your dog's aggressiveness could not be contained, and you wondered what in the heck the dog was getting so hysterical about. In the end, not seeing the world as your pet sees it leaves you to believe there is nothing there. Let's take that same situation and adjust it a little by first giving you a feeling that there is something in the room with you prior to the dog acting so territorial. How do you react to this? Are you nervous or do you feel threatened? Let's change the situation altogether, with a totally different scenario. Let's say the dog loves playing with tennis balls and you are walking together in a park, when all of a sudden, the dog jets into the bushes and finds a ball buried in the deep grass, which moments earlier was invisible to the human eye.

Would you ever say the dog has a disability because it has a stronger sense of smell than yours? Even though science has proven some dogs have an olfactory system that gives them smell capabilities two hundred times greater than man and they have hearing capabilities that enable them to hear in multiple range levels different from what man is capable of hearing in, when our dogs react to things that are seemingly invisible to human senses, we usually discount it as "the dog being goofy."

To bring the dog back under your control and to eliminate the odd behavior, you try to distract it and bring it back into terms you are more comfortable with by pulling out a dog treat and stuffing it in its mouth to shut it up.

Many people actually end up reprimanding the dog for acting aggressively at things their "masters" are not able to see. Dogs, after being punished for trying to alert the family to what it recognizes as an intruder, must think the family is thoroughly confused with their response of yelling at them or tossing them outside after they risk their lives trying a give perfect warning. This is most definitely why Fluffy often demonstrates poor behavior later in life; in fact, it has been proven that many dogs will revert to eating disorders, alcoholism, and butt dragging across grandparents' carpets as a way to deal with these past times of confusion.

This difference between the dog and their human counterparts relates directly to my ability to see what others cannot see. My problem is since my vision enables me to see auras and energy levels, I also see the same apparitions that the family pets see. Many times, I will see them before the dog, so I can at least warn everyone that the dog is about to go a little wild. This pre-attack warning is appreciated by everyone in my proximity, but it nevertheless evokes many questions. The problem with these questions is I cannot answer most of them. I know nothing about ghosts; I cannot talk to ghosts; I cannot hear ghostly screams; I cannot feel their presence, nor do I know who they were when they originally walked the earth. I can only see that something is around and is creating an energy flow, but I have no real answers as to what it is.

Our old historical town has a rich history full of old ghost stories told by many people who claim not only to see the apparitions, but also to know who died and is now haunting things. One of the oddest homes in town is directly across the street from our house; it is listed in the national registry as "one of the most haunted houses in the country." This particular house has a terrible history of having housed many Chinese women who were brought to California as sex slaves during the gold rush days. These women worked in the sex-trade business as prostitutes, and each evening after the brothels were closed, they were locked in the basement of the home and were kept under guard until the following day. Their lives were horrible, and they lived in tight quarters in a squalid existence. Their lives were tortured, and their existence was meager. Most of these women carried and died of disease. The owner of the home was married, and they had a child. Both the wife and the child died from diseases carried by the women in the basement, leaving the man a broken and disgraced individual. Upon the death of the wife and child, and surely overwhelmed by his own conscience, the man draped a rope over the main beam in the carriage house and hung himself until the last bit of air was snuffed from his worthless body. Ever since that event, his old house has been documented by many owners and passersby as a haven for ghosts.

With a history as cold as this, it is no wonder why so many people report seeing ghostly images. This house being so close in proximity to my home, I also see my share of interesting sights, but I rarely report my findings because I have found it serves no usefulness for me or my family to report what others just cannot see. The uniqueness of this home though is it has the boldness to share its energy with the average individual by opening and closing windows and window shades, turning on the furnace, slamming doors and starting fires in the fireplace, all while no one is at home.

On several evenings, while we were entertaining out-of-town guests, we would discuss the unusual events of the neighboring home while meandering home from a night on the town. We would reach our house, and as we were looking at the neighbor's home, things would get a little crazy. One evening, it became so obvious that whatever you call them—ghosts, energy levels, or things of that sort—were ruling the home in a display of discomfort and were causing so much noise and chaos that the local police had to be called in to quiet the situation. When the police arrived, they witnessed the windows opening and closing in various parts of the home, multiple window shades opening and closing simultaneously, and smoke and sparks coming out of the fireplace. All of this was happening while the owners of the home were away. The police called the fire department to investigate the matter of the smoke and sparks coming out of the home, since the owners were away, and upon further inspection, they not only couldn't find an active fire causing the sparks and smoke, but they couldn't even find any ashes. Upon closing their inspection, the police and fire crews said, "We hate going into the home, because it always smells like death."

Even with all of what most people would call "evidence of ghostly presences" being there, my logical mind still tells me there are answers that are being overlooked. I may be wrong, as I don't profess to be an expert in these matters, but it's at least all very entertaining.

So here I was embarking on an early morning stroll through town feeling uneasy about something that I just couldn't put my finger on. As I rounded the curve in the road that leads to the inner section of town, I saw a large aura of someone sitting in the distance. As I got closer, I could see it was a man on one of the benches; his legs were crossed and he was swinging his foot back and forth. His clothes were clean and pressed, but something seemed odd about the style, although not so different that I would say anything. He was a lean man, and even though it was a chillier than usually morning, he was lightly dressed. I would have been shivering violently on a cold morning such as this if I were dressed like him, but he looked very comfortable, almost like someone who is resting on a bench in a park on a warm sunny day.

As I approached him, he offered a silent nod of greeting to me, so I said, "Hello," to him. I thought it quite odd that someone was sitting there in the middle of the night and acting as lively and happy as though this were the middle of the day.

As I continued walking past his spot, he called me by name, "Bob, how's your family doing?"

I had recently lost my father and sister to the sickle of the grim reaper, so I thought the question was quite odd. He then asked me specifically, "How are Ed and Wendy doing?"

He knew my father's and sister's names! With that, I spun around from my forward trajectory and looked him straight in the eyes, trying to figure out who this person was. My father had only lived in town for a short while before passing away a few years earlier, and my sister, who had suffered from a lifelong condition and had passed away only a few months earlier, had never lived in town. This person was acting as though we had known each other for a lifetime. I wanted to know who he was and how he knew this intimate information, so as I reeled around and looked at him, I asked those very questions. "How do we know each other, and how did you know those names?"

When I looked him in the eyes, I noticed something very strange: his eyes were dark as mud. I felt very uneasy yet very comfortable in his presence at the same time.

He responded, "Yes, you know me. You've known me all of your life."

I was still very curious about how he knew my sister by name since she had never been to my town and in fact had been living in a care facility a couple of hundred miles away. I thought it very odd for this person to know anything about her. I had been acting as custodian for her affairs after my father's death, but for anyone to know this in my town would have been impossible. So I asked the man in a very shaky voice, "Did you know my sister too?"

He responded by saying, "Thank you for helping your sister; she needed you, and you were there."

I really didn't know how to respond to that, as I didn't recognize him and I certainly didn't want to embarrass myself or him by suggesting that I didn't know him, especially since he'd just said that we had known each other all of our lives. He obviously knew about my sister, but I had to ask the question again, "Where have we met before?"

I will never forget his response for as long as I live. He said, "I knew you when you were born, and you knew me. I knew you when you first rode a bike, and you knew me. I knew you when you got married and then had your daughter, and you knew me. I knew you when your father and sister died, and you knew me, and I'll be around anytime you become happy or sad or need me."

With that, I figured I was going nuts, and I couldn't even talk anymore, so I turned and walked down the street without saying another word, just shaking my head. I thought for a second and said to myself, "Okay, what's the logical answer here? I must be sleepwalking or something. What the hell is happening?"

I had walked about fifty feet and turned to go back to the man to ask more questions, but he was gone. To this day, I have no idea who that man was. The more disturbing comment came days later when I ran into my neighbors on the street. They were curious as to why they'd seen me walking into town the other day at 3:00 a.m., so I told them I just couldn't sleep. Their next question floored me when they asked, "Who was the guy following you as you walked into town that morning?"

Being one who doesn't like this type of attention, I simply responded, "An old friend."

CHAPTER 13

Testing My Vision at the University

The morning was colder than usual in Southern California. The air was damp and heavy, which created a gray fogginess that filled the air. The steady breeze was just strong enough to create a chilling feeling that caused the residents to develop goose bumps. People familiar with the cooler temperatures understood what it meant to see these cold-weather permutations appear on their bodies and were fine with them; however, those inhabitants who had never ventured out of Southern California's consistently warm climate became frightened at the very sight of this aberration. Many had heard of cool weather, some had even seen pictures of it in magazines or on television, but no one had ever detailed the body's reaction to cold weather for them.

What were these bumps? Were these bumps infectious? Could children catch these bumps from their parents? To the native SoCal (as they referred to themselves) residents these questions had to be answered and fast. The hospital ERs were filled beyond capacity as individuals swarmed to find out what was happening. Since many doctors had never seen these goose bumps over their careers in Southern California, they decided to fly in several experts in skin-disease matters from the Office of Disease Control, headquartered in San Francisco, to help identify and control the outbreak. As soon as these experts from the cold region of San Francisco climbed off the plane wearing heavy coats, you just knew there was going to be an issue, and there was, *immediately*. There really was! The experts were lost for words. What do you say to someone whose life experiences render him naive to the rest of the word?

These same SoCal doctors who had to fly in the NorCA doctors just to identify what *goose bumps* were, were about to start measuring my sight abilities so they could report their findings to the rest of the medical world. They would give their answers and theories regarding my special visual capacity. They would finally have the answers we were all looking for—well, the answers that *almost* all of us were looking for. I knew from my own life experiences that it was usually much better to traverse through life without saying too much, as Miranda has always been correct that whatever you say and do "can and will be held against you."

Normally, I couldn't care less about the freaky goings-on about doctors or their "unusual" findings. For the first time in my life, I was growing fearful of the medical world. I still didn't care about the SoCal's medical findings about my condition, yet I was very apprehensive, as logic told me these same doctors would be examining me and the world and, more important, *I* would have to live with their reports and conclusions, good or bad.

Because of my apprehension, I didn't sleep well the night before my hospital visit. As a result of my lack of sleep, I was grumpy and very quiet during my visit. My family was quite concerned with my quiet, introverted behavior, as they couldn't ever recall a time in my past when I had been speechless.

I really didn't care what these doctors were about to find with my vision, because it wasn't going to change a thing for me except that people might at least understand my visual differences better and maybe their newfound information would be useful for others. What I did not want to deal with was the constant testing, prodding, and poking I was about to undergo as doctors and machines all the while would be looking at me sideways like I was some kind of lab rat. I don't mind doctors as a general rule, as long as they are working on someone else. Doctors are a very peculiar breed; they feel empowered to ask you thousands of questions, but as soon as you ask them just one question, their attitude changes from calm to combative. Since doctors are highly trained with years of medical experience, they believe you should simply trust their findings as correct. Asking a doctor a simple question is interpreted by them as asking them to prove their answers, and they do not appreciate this in anyway. Asking too many questions could cause you to wake up three days later with your frontal lobe removed. So I just shut up and let them prod away.

Human beings have an unshakable ability to use pack mentality and team up against anything or anyone that can be defined as "different." This mentality is ever present in everyone's everyday lives and is the root reason why the world will always suffer from gossip, racial prejudice, and bullying. People take the easy path of competing by looking for the differences others have and then knocking them down instead of taking the more difficult path of becoming better human beings themselves. Until humans start celebrating their differences as what unites them in life's groups, we will always be destined to aim for and achieve life's minimum standards and results.

I digress, but I want to make sure that you understand that I understood exactly why I was requested to be at the university. It wasn't to improve my differences and solve some of life's mysteries as much as it was to put me in the "odd" box where I could be controlled. I had everything to lose and nothing to gain by going through their process, but in life, you sometimes have to acquiesce to others or the community around you can create a living hell for you.

These people who live under the group mentality exist everywhere around us, and even though we may not realize it to be true or hope that it's not true, people in the medical field are no different from others and share the same prejudices in life that point to the "if it's different, it's weird" theories. People with this same attitude would be measuring my "different" qualities shortly, and I would have to live with their findings. If they reported this information as being odd to my family in a negative way, I could deal with it, as I would have no other choices. If my differences got out into my immediate circle of friends, nothing would change because they have always been aware of my unique abilities. What I wasn't sure about was what would happen if my unusual features got out into the world beyond my immediate friends and family. What would be the results of strangers knowing about my different visual abilities? Would the world be okay with this? Would I be chastised by my own community? Would I be placed in the freak category? Would my family and friends suffer the same fate? Many questions circle through your head during these processes, but your life becomes part of the process once it starts; there is no turning back, so you go through the test, and you react according to the testers' results.

The university had booked an early morning appointment for my vision test. I had no idea what the school had prepared for me with these tests, and I entered the facility ready to have a quick eye exam and get the hell out of there. Did I mention how much I hate visiting doctors' offices? Hate 'em *a lot*! I have always wondered why some doctors' offices have "No Soliciting" signs on their front doors? Do they really have to work at keeping people away? That's like posting a sign in the viewing area of a mortuary that says, "No Loitering." Does it really need to be said?

When I stepped into the office, I quickly learned that which followed would be more than just another day. When I arrived at the testing center, they sat me down in a large office with a drop-top table filled with disassembled puzzle games and asked me to wait for the doctor. My mind hates clutter almost as much as doctors' offices and here was a table filled with clutter. To take my mind off of waiting for the doctor, I participated in reassembling the puzzles. Unbeknownst to me, these puzzles had been left there purposely to see my response and were designed as a measurement of intellect. To me, the surroundings were boring, and I had thought nothing of the surroundings other than noticing that I was the only one present in the room. I waited roughly one minute before boredom overtook my mind, and I began working on the puzzles. It's important to note that by my standards, I thought that I had acted with great restraint by waiting a full minute before becoming a tad bored. Anyway, these puzzles were very easy for me to reassemble, and I had completed what I thought was the task: straightening up a bunch of clutter. Upon my completion of the puzzles, the doctor and a few assistants entered the room and revealed that the task was actually a measured study, and they further told me that the time I waited before starting the project and the time it took me to complete the project set records. Also, upon completing the reassembly work, the doctor also divulged to me that my progress had been viewed though a two-way mirror. My view point was very different, as I would tell you the doctor's office was a mess; they had left toys strewn all over the table, and people spied on you there and then rushed in, gave you accolades, and told you how smart you were for cleaning up their messes! I really hated doctor's offices after that.

The doctor then gave me a standard IQ test to complete. Obviously, I was very quizzical as to what this had to do with the sight test I was there to complete and was told that the IQ test was standard procedure for someone who was about to be tested on the Kirlian camera. The university was performing multiple tests on me to identify whether or not there was a correlation between intelligence and the ability to see things differently than most people.

So like a good student, I completed the IQ test as just another thing that needed to be completed as a standard operation. Thinking nothing further about the test and not really caring too much about it or the results, I went to work on it. It should be noted that I do not believe in tests of this nature, because I feel any such test can be manipulated by the test taker. Regardless, I finished the test quickly and without fuss and gave it to the doctor. Apparently, the doctor thought I had finished the exam too quickly and reviewed it for completion. The doctor believed that I had purposely skimmed the test and randomly filled in A, B, C, or D bubbles to get the test over with, so she started asking me random questions from the test and checking to see if the answers I was now giving her matched the answers that I had just entered in the answer space. Since I had actually read the exam and provided my answers, she concluded that I had actually done the test.

Upon checking my answers with the master, she concluded that I must have taken the exam before, because most of my answers were correct and there would have been no way I could have gotten so many questions correct by simply guessing. The results indicated that I had a much higher than average IQ, but to prove my point that these tests are all flawed, I should tell you that the doctor had found a couple of errors in my answers but all of my answers were actually correct and the answer guide that the doctor was using was actually incorrect. I should also point out that I'm not egotistical, self-centered, or overconfident, just simply always right about everything and anything. In fact, if you don't believe me, I don't care. Anyway, apparently, if I had been born an idiot, my visual abilities would not have developed.

Before testing my vision and comparing their finding to a Kirlian camera, the doctors and scientists had me take a standard IQ test, I assumed because their findings would point to a low IQ and would somehow prove I was a nut. The results came back higher than average, but my results weren't so freakishly high that I was mentally imbalanced and they weren't low either. In their summation, I could actually walk and talk normally, so something else had to be triggering my belief that I could see auras.

Since my IQ tests were within their "normal" range, their next exam would include the standard brain wave tests. The electroencephalograph (EEG) measures brain electrical activity. Doctors know what normal brain activity looks like, so anytime something wacky or unusual is going on, the doctors start sticking a bunch of electrodes to your head that lead to a bunch of computers. This test is usually done for people suffering from seizures or when they want to see if a drug addict has fried his or her brains. The EEG points out detectable abnormalities in the brain. This test gets your attention, because if the findings are bad and they decide your melon has suffered too much damage, I believe they just turn up the energy and stick you in a rubber room where you can't cause any trouble.

So after the doctors greased me up and connected all of the diodes, I told them to "hit the juice." They all kind of looked at me a little sideways and started their tests. I guess I had been incorrect about what would happen during this test, as I received no shocks or jolts of electricity, and I never even blacked out. I was disappointed that these tests were not very traumatic, as I had prepared myself emotionally for the worst. I guess I should have asked more questions of the doctors!

At the conclusion of these tests, all findings were negative. At first, I thought a negative result was bad—really bad. The doctors had to have found something positive in my head, but nope, their findings were 100 percent negative. How could this be? There had to be something in my skull; after all, I had driven myself to the appointment, talking on my cell phone as I went; I'd dressed myself and fed myself. Wow, 100 percent negative! I decided there had to be a mistake with the findings, so I broke my own rule and asked the doctors a question. My question was quickly answered with the affirmation that negative findings were good, as they meant there were no problems. Phew, that was a relief! I can't believe people don't ask their doctors more questions!

Well, good IQ, negative EEG, I thought I was on the home stretch and was going to be released back to the general population. The doctors and scientists had different ideas though. It's funny how when you do well on medical tests and procedures, more and more doctors and scientists start showing up. Pretty soon, if you are getting great results, you have all of the doctors. I guess doctors don't like being around sick people either, because they were all with me and my tests were showing great results. In fact, the doctors, scientists, and I were having so much fun that they decided we should play games and do puzzles together. Their parents never educated them on how games should be played with others though, and I made the determination right then and there that I would never play games with doctors again once I got out of there.

Their idea of fun was to bring in a bunch of brain-twister tests and puzzles and have you put them together. First, they would give you one or two, and you'd put them together. They would immediately bust them up and mix them up with other puzzles. I was soon putting together about twenty scrambled puzzles that had all been mixed together. The doctors and scientists would leave the room and stand staring at me through a two-way mirror as I put their puzzles back together. They finally stopped doing this after I told them I was bored and ready to leave and that I knew they were watching me through the mirror, as I could see all of their auras. Their conclusions were that I was a great puzzle solver, as I broke the current records set previously for putting the puzzles back together.

Finally, they decided to compare my visual abilities with what they saw on a Kirlian camera and a biofeedback aura imaging machine. This was new to me, as I had never heard of these things before. When they revealed what the cameras and tests could do, I was very excited, as what I had been telling everyone that I was able to see would for the very first time in my life be proven, and I would be vindicated for all of my doubters. I was very surprised that the doctors hadn't started with these tests instead of trying to prove I was nuts first.

The people performing the test ushered out many of the doctors and only allowed three of the people to stay in the room to monitor the results. These three people were highly skilled, and before they performed the test, they spent quite a lot of time telling me about what they were about to do and also warning me about the risks of disclosing the possible findings. I didn't care; I was ready to have my world proven.

The doctors performed their tests flawlessly, determining how much detail I was able to provide compared to their cameras and instruments. Their toys were good, as they measured energy levels, aura colors, and visual differences between the things they tested, but my results were much stronger, as I was also able to properly interpret what I saw and their machines couldn't.

Everything was going very well with the tests until we got closer to the conclusion, and I told one of the doctors whom I had witnessed all day as having a weak aura on his left side to go get tested. He laughed my comments off until one of the other doctors who had apparently heard my remarks pointed the aura camera at him and clicked off a couple of photos. These photos confirmed my observations. The doctor who was photographed with a weak aura was out of the office in a hurry to get further medical tests.

The excitement and stir that I created for this doctor ended my day of puzzles, tests, Kirlian machines, doctors, and everything else they could think of throwing at me, and I was finally going home. I was quite exhausted after a *long* day and was more than ready to get out of there. I couldn't help feeling relieved about how these test results were finally going to squelch all of the naysayers who had doubted me for one reason or another. I could only smile to myself as I would be able to rub these results in their faces once and for all. What a great time this would be. One problem, these results would not be released to my doubters; instead, they were released to the government intelligence agencies, as I was now considered a potential threat. Nobody told me this though; I would learn about it by accident, but I will say, your life changes fast when this sort of thing happens.

CHAPTER 14

Uh-Oh, Running Again!

Several months had passed since the Seattle incident, and I hadn't heard a word from anyone; I hadn't seen any cars with suspicious people parked outside of my house, restaurants I was visiting, or hotels I was staying at, and it was wonderful. I thought that the last incident was so dramatic that maybe, just maybe, everyone was through with me.

After a meal in town, my wife and I decided to walk through town and window-shop to see if anything interesting was on display. That was when I noticed for the first time in many months, that the hope that my sight abilities were no longer of interest to anyone and my family and I wouldn't be bothered anymore was vastly incorrect.

While looking into one of the storefront windows, I noticed the reflection of a man in a car paying close attention to our movements. I didn't say anything to my wife, but I proceeded along the row of businesses in a hyper vigilant manner making sure to keep a nonchalant eye on where this man was. I was also trying to see if others were acting unusually odd or perched in unusual places. As far as I could tell, there were at least three men and one woman who appeared suspiciously out of place.

We kept up our pace through town and eventually went into one of the wine-tasting businesses to get an after-dinner drink. It was in there that I told my wife what was happening. I told her to stay calm. We knew most of the merchants in town, and we also knew all of the back alley walkways, which actually operated somewhat like a backroom in a mall. The alleyway behind many of these businesses allowed merchants to exit their stores without going directly out a backdoor, which makes it incredibly difficult for someone to simply park out back of a store and catch you if that was their intent.

I told my wife I would stay at the wine shop and wait it out to see who was following us this time. I had her leave through the back maze and call one of her friends to pick her up. I would pick her up from her friend's house later, once the situation at hand was resolved. She left without incident.

People who are following you hate situations like this, because they have no patience and waiting to them is hell. When you take too long to exit, they think you sneaked out and eventually come looking for you. It usually only takes about an hour before they come sniffing around the grounds. They always walk past the front window several times to see if they can see you, and when they can't, they finally come in. Because I knew this, I purposely sat in the far back corner of the room knowing they wouldn't be able to see me through the tinted windows and would have to come in.

I thought back to the day in Seattle and actually missed not having the team that had followed my every step for years, as I had learned they had also provided me and my family with an amount of protection. My thoughts were on these new people following me; I wondered if they were friends or foes. I decided I would stay put and find out shortly.

Uh-Oh, Running Again!

I saw the woman pass by the front window several times during a fifteen-minute period before she finally entered the room. I knew she couldn't see me well, as I was sitting quietly in the back of the room. I was baffled, as she never really tried to find me once she entered the room and only quickly glanced around the room and then positioned herself at a table directly in the front of the room where she obviously was very interested in the happenings going on outside the business.

Seconds later, a head-on accident took place directly in front of the window as one car appeared to drive directly into another oncoming car. Just as fast as the crash occurred, a storm of people on the sidewalk rushed in and picked up the inhabitants of the car that had crashed into the other. They were handcuffed and hauled off in a van. It happened so quickly that witnesses really couldn't account for everything that had gone on.

From past experiences, I knew what had just happened. The US team had just intercepted a threat against me from an international intelligence team that I had no idea was in the area.

The woman at the front window turned and walked directly back to me. She said, "I'm surprised that you weren't being more careful." I said nothing as she walked out the back door into the maze of doorways leading out back, I assumed she was heading for a waiting car.

I thought to myself, *what the hell was that? What just happened here?* I had thought I was so smart and had everything figured out, and now all of this. I knew one thing for sure: I didn't need to wait around for the local police to show up; I just needed to get my wife and go home. She would never believe this story. I didn't think I believed it myself, and I'd just seen it with my own eyes.

I knew one thing for sure though: my guardian angels were back, and it felt pretty damn good. I still didn't like all of the running around and secrecy my family had to deal with, as different people always wanted my assistance for things like interrogations or looking at high-ranking politicians and generals to see if they had weak auras, which ultimately showed signs of their deception, but I knew with the US intelligence teams watching our backs, we were probably safe. I also played it differently with this new team, as I knew they had a tough occupation and they really didn't need me being an extra thorn in their asses while they did their jobs.

CHAPTER 15

Casino Night—"You Wouldn't Be Bluffing Me, Would You?"

Ever since I was a young boy, I have always loved the casinos. Who wouldn't, with all of the glitzy lights; the enormous artwork hanging on the walls; the shiny chrome slot machines with all of the flashing colors that hypnotized you and pulled you into their warm, lustful atmosphere and then rewarded your solidarity and allegiance by yelling out to you with a triumphant "Ding, ding, ding!" of their bells recognizing and announcing to everyone that you were a winner; and the soft felt of the boardroom game tables with the card dealers dressed in black coat suits one would normally only use and see on special days or at special events, such as weddings or award meetings. The rooms were carpeted with meandering floral designs in contrasting and warm colors that ran to the walls where they exploded into lush, mosaic wallpaper designs that stretched up to ceiling art leaving the casual observer to ponder the question of whether Leonardo himself had just finished another great work of art. Enjoying these great halls with their cavalier yet romantic styles, where pure oxygen was pumped in to keep everyone awake, alive, and happy, was just one part of the casino experience. These palaces of excitement were designed to provide joy and warmth to the constant flow of money-bearing guests as they entered happy with their cash and left with a happy experience, but not with their money. Casinos offered a unique opportunity for people to give away their money without feeling bad.

I was never hyped into wanting to lose money, as I never felt good about those types of experiences; in fact, I can't remember ever losing money from gambling with others. My winning streak, which dated back to my earliest memories, had nothing to do with luck; rather, it was a direct result of my visual differences. From my first memories of being introduced to casinos as a ten-year-old boy, I remember my dad telling me to stand within eyesight of him and to give him a thumbs-up sign if the person he was playing cards against was bluffing his bet. I was also instructed to stay on the walkways outside of the immediate table areas because casinos seemed to have issues with ten-year-olds roaming the gaming areas. His final bit of advice to me was to stay away from the casino security people.

It's funny when you look back on your life and realize how much you as a ten-year-old were capable of accomplishing with little instruction. Anyway, I did as I was told and became very good at our little game of hold the thumbs-up sign, ditch the guards, hold the thumbs-up sign, and ditch the guards. This would only last a short time before they recognized my father was the one focusing on my actions. They also realized that my father was winning a large amount of money in a short period of time, and nothing attracts security in a casino quicker than people who are winning. Anyway, we were usually asked to leave quite urgently. They were always nice to me, but my father had to learn how to roll quickly and swiftly through front doors and across the rigid concrete entrances. He became very good at the exit process, and I believe he actually started picking the casinos based on how easily the front doors opened and what kinds of materials were on the outside of the front doors; his preference was soft carpeting out front.

My father was very sharp and always an opportunist. When he first learned of my visual differences, he ignored them, as I believe he felt they would only lead to embarrassing situations between him and his friends, our neighbors, and other lines of our family. He would never acknowledge my difference publically, and if it came up in outside conversations, he would laugh it off almost as if to say, "Kids are just goofy sometimes." He did not ever want to discuss it outside the house. When it was just immediate family around, he was exactly the opposite of his public persona. I became the lab rat, and he was the mad scientist. He was determined to understand my differences completely and have the greatest scientist in the world both acknowledge and confirm my visual differences and the greatness I possessed, which could only have come from his genes. I didn't mind, because he was funny to me and I just liked hanging out with him.

After years of trying to figure out why my eyes worked the way they did, only to zero in on no answers, he finally gave up looking for solutions until one day when an event caused a light bulb to abruptly go on in his head. My family always played card games, and my father was an old-school poker player. He loved cards, and I believe he used to see himself as Doc Holliday sitting around a smoky table in the Old West playing in the final round of the evening with the pot in the middle of the table chocking itself with a pile of gold, silver, and paper money. All of the players would be staring at each other, watching every move to see if the other players were bluffing or cheating. If they were bluffing, they were about to get called on their move; if they were cheating, they were about to get shot dead at the table. Either way, my father felt he was the king of poker tables and he would own the souls of anyone who ever dared to sit at his table.

My father only suffered from one setback as a poker player: he couldn't read people. I don't mean that he couldn't read people who were good at hiding their emotions like you'd find in great card smiths; I mean he couldn't read people, period. If someone had a sign posted on their

foreheads that read, "I'm bluffing, and I have crap for a hand, but I'm going to keep betting just to drive up the bet and to scare the other players
away," my dad would be the first to fold his hand and throw away a sure
win. This all changed one evening when my family was playing cards.

We were playing different types of poker games, and I kept winning
all of the hands that I could possibly win, and I kept folding when I didn't
have the winning hand. When there was a hand that others were betting
on where their hands were okay but not great, I would run up the bet and
they would eventually get out as I kept pushing the bets up. My perfor-
mance was so strong and my chip count was so large that my family members started thinking that I was somehow cheating. As my father pushed
the issue, he started realizing that I would simply look at the people when
they got their cards from the dealer, and my eyes would dart around them
focusing on their outlines. He asked me why I was doing this, so I told
him the truth that when a player got poor cards, he or she was obviously
not comfortable. This discomfort caused people to have thin auras. On
the other hand, when someone had a great hand, he or she became very
comfortable and his or her aura became much wider than usual. Average
hands produced auras that varied in thickness between the two. When I
saw a thick aura, I folded; when it was thin, they usually folded. I really
enjoyed seeing the middle-size auras, because I knew they'd stay in for a
while, and I would try to see how many chips I could get those players to
put in before they left. I told my dad I liked the chips, and it was fun to
take them from everyone all the time.

After explaining my strategy, I looked around the table and saw many
blank faces with mouths wide open. Upon my announcements, my brother immediately laid his cards down and left the table, and to this date, he
has never played cards with me again. My father's response was quite different though; he became a rapid-fire police interrogator, and I somehow
assumed the role of a perpetrator needing to be grilled. Knowing that the
family had stayed in the casinos in Lake Tahoe a hundred times when we
would go skiing in the mountains and that we had walked past the card

tables and thousands of poker games, he asked me, "Were you ever able to see any of their auras?"

"Yes," I told him, "I saw them all."

He then asked, "Are you still able to see auras in strangers?"

"Yes," I told him again. "I can see the people's auras in the casinos better than I can see our family's, I guess because they are playing for money, and we are only playing for chips. I think the money is very important to them, as their auras really react to whatever cards they are holding."

The conclusion of this interrogation left me somewhat confused, as my dad asked me to go get my coat and my mom said I would not be going to get my coat. I'm glad my mom was there, because it was too warm for a coat. I didn't want to go get it. They sure disagreed on that coat though, because they fought like crazy over it.

My parents eventually stopped fighting about the coat, but they would fight whenever my dad and I would return from trips. My dad would set up fishing, camping, and kite-flying trips for us, but a lot of times, something would happen and the trips would get changed at the last minute. We'd end up at a casino as a result. When we'd get home, my mom would ask how the trip went, and I'd tell her it was cancelled. She would then immediately start yelling at Dad. I felt bad for the guy; after all, he'd set up all of these trips and they'd get cancelled at the last minute, and then my mom would yell at him. Talk about a no-win situation.

Since my dad was always in trouble lately, I figured the least I could do was to help him with his poker, so I'd go with him to the casinos and hold up my thumbs until they would toss my father to the curb and tell us we were not allowed to come back. We would scurry along to another casino where we would again be tossed out and asked not to come back. This went on for some time until we had been removed from all of the casinos. In fact, a couple of the casinos tossed us out twice. This would happen because my father believed that if you didn't show up for a while, they'd forget about the previous encounter and you would be good to go. The problem was that when they did put everything together and realized who we were and this had happened before, they were not as kind show-ing my dad out the front doors. The first time they tossed him out, they at least opened the doors, but the second time, they actually opened the doors by throwing him through them. They even swatted me out the front doors for my second visits using brooms. I was always laughing at myself and the situation, because it just never felt real to me. I felt like we were in a Laurel and Hardy slapstick comedy movie.

The newness eventually wore off, and my father got tired of being tossed through doors and couldn't take anymore arguments with my mom over my wearing coats, so he stopped taking me to all of the casinos. I still can't figure out why they fought so much over that stupid coat. Hell, it wasn't even a nice coat. Anyway, over time, things quieted down; he wouldn't discuss my differences with anyone outside the house, and I moved along in life like any other kid. My differences came roaring back to life though when I was in college, as many nights were spent playing poker for beer, food, and money. However, it should be pointed out that there was far more beer, some food, and very little money during my college days. Either way, I liked winning whatever anyone had that they wanted to play cards for. So I started playing poker again, and I started winning a lot—make that everything. At first, my roommates and friends hated me since they kept losing to me. Their parents stopped liking me as well, as they ultimately had to pay to replace everything their kids had lost. I believe I am the only college-aged kid whose friends' parents told them they were not allowed to play with me anymore.

College was the first time I had thought about the old days when my dad had me holding up hand signals in the casinos, telling him when to bet and when to fold, and I realized what our fatal flaw had been. Since my dad couldn't see the auras, he had to use the abilities of a ten-year-old kid. The guards wouldn't have seen him if I hadn't been hanging around the outer areas. So if I went to the casinos and used my visual differences while playing poker myself, I couldn't get into any trouble, because I technically wouldn't be cheating. I'm slow sometimes, but the brokeness associated with college life can motivate the slow to move along at a very different pace, and since I was extremely broke during college, I had a great motivation for a better pace.

So off I went to the casinos to test my hypothesis with all of the money I had to my name. Well, actually, I only had thirty dollars, and the casino said I needed one hundred to join their smallest tournament. I begged and borrowed seventy dollars from a few friends and off I went.

I entered the tournament against roughly a hundred other poker players and won my first event and a couple thousand dollars. The event was small, the people were horrible, and the room smelled like dead goats. I had no idea what dead goats smelled like, but I was sure if there were a bunch of dead goats, they would have smelled bad like that poker room. It smelled so bad that I almost gave up my quest to win money playing cards. I went back to more and more tournaments, winning most of them and creating a name for myself. I was now being watched and filmed by casino security. This didn't bother me at all, because if I were in their shoes, I would want to know how this person was winning so much money as well. I would laugh to myself though and wonder, with all of the sophisticated security that casinos had nowadays, if they were ever able to piece my trail back to the ten-year-old kid and his father who used to get tossed out of the casinos?

Well, I kept playing and kept winning. I would get tossed out of some of the casinos under the accusation of cheating; this was usually done in order to avoid paying me out on my winnings and is quite common among some of the big-name casinos. If they think you're cheating, you have to prove that you are not, and good luck getting someone to believe you. Being a card shark is not exactly an admirable or respectable way to make a living, and it's hard to get people to believe you if you work in this profession even if you are honest.

Other casinos didn't toss me out; instead they would invite me to play private poker tournaments in upstairs penthouse rooms. It was always very interesting to me that I never saw one microphone or camera in all of the years that I played poker, yet I knew they were there because there was absolutely no other motivation for them to invite me to these matches unless they were going to film me in order to find out my cheating methods.

After a while, the game of poker become old and as stale as the years of cigarette smoke that filled the casino air. The cards became boring to look at, and the conversations become so repetitive over the years that I knew what the new players were going to ask before anything came out of their mouths. You know the type and quality of people the card players hung around. Some of their girlfriends were pretty, while most were average looking, but under their skin, most were tramps looking for a free ride. They acted cute to get their way with guys who were so pathetic, so unimpressive that they had never learned how to tell women like that to take a hike. I used to wonder if these guys would ever grow a backbone in life or if they would all die alone and broke, sleeping under a park bench because they never had enough guts or confidence to shoo the wretched sluts away.

Don't get me wrong, when I was first playing cards, I used to enjoy watching these girls come around and interact with their boyfriends just to get some money from them while the tournaments were going on. I would laugh as I listened to the exchanges that took place, and I used to laugh at the guys when their girlfriends would show up and realize their guy had lost the match. The girlfriends of these guys would start a fight to break off relations with the guys who lost, and almost in the same breath, they would be making moves to get in good with the winners because they were not interested in the guys; they were only interested in their winnings. This would go on and on, and after being greeted by these "gracious" women many times and knowing that they disgusted me more than being sprayed by a family of skunks, I used to mock them with their own shallowness. I would give them twenty dollars to go to the valet to retrieve my car, and I would tell them I would meet them there and we would go for a drink or some dinner. I would tell them to tell the valet I had a nice, but common car like a black Mercedes or a blue BMW and for them to wait for me in the car and I would be right out. They would go to get the car, and the valet would have absolutely no idea which car they were looking for, because I had made the whole thing up. The girls would argue with the valets because they were being told by the valets that they were unsure of what car was mine. The girls, feeling too embarrassed that they couldn't complete the simple task of retrieving my car, which again never existed, would take so much time arguing with the valets that I always had enough time to exit a different way. By the time the girls finally got the nerve to come back into the casino to report the problem of locating my car, I would be gone. I always followed the gamblers number one rule for anyone that's a headliner; you never park in the casino's garage where you will be playing, too much potential risk.

So between the smoke, the conversations, and the girls, I walked out (wasn't thrown out) of my last casino years ago, and I never looked back. I feel I'm one of the lucky ones, since during those days, I never lost my direction, my money, or my classy expectations in life. The only thing I wish I could have learned during my card-playing days was what the hell my parents were fighting about with my coat all the time; that still bugs me.

CHAPTER 16

Myth of the "Magic Glasses"

Ever since I was thirteen years old, I have worked. I've had many jobs. My parents always wanted me to keep busy. My friends' families wanted me kept busy. The fathers of the girls that I knew wanted me kept busy. It seemed that everyone who knew me wanted to keep me occupied. All I cared about was just having a couple of extra bucks for spending money.

I had the normal fill of many different jobs during my school years, such as paperboy, horse stall cleaner, busboy, waiter, and cook, and all seemed very normal. I had the proper youthful attitude that all jobs were as boring as their creators had intended them to be. After learning how to hide my yawns from my bosses during my first several jobs, I finally found my calling after I took my first sales job.

I never knew how much I would enjoy sales until I learned about the skills involved with selling. I learned very early on in my sales career that there was a real skill to learn with selling and individuals who took the time to learn how sales and the process really worked would become very successful, both financially and otherwise. I also learned that most people who became salespeople did so not because they had any intent of studying the craft or becoming good salespeople, but because they heard salespeople made the most money and anyone could be successful in sales. They went into the sales profession for the wrong reasons and failed. Then they went through life bashing salespeople and their profession out of jealousy and spite because of their own failures. This is very common, as there are far fewer successful salespeople than unsuccessful ones. It is very hard to find a salesperson that chose the very difficult occupation that a sales career offers with the right understanding and the hopes of someday mastering the skill.

I have always understood the opportunities that exist and the financial reward potential from having a successful sales career, and I have also had the personal fortune of making multimillions of dollars from sales. However, I am one of those rare individuals who joined the sales world not because of the potential fortunes to be made, but because it offered me, with my odd visual differences, the opportunity and personal satisfaction to further my understanding of people and how their individual behavior patterns mirrored or differed from what I saw in them from their energy levels and auras. Sales gave me a direct insight channel to follow when studying the difference between how I expected people to act based on what I saw in their auras and how they really behaved.

During my initial sales years, I learned how to read my audiences far beyond normal body-language sales reads. I learned that by seeing prospects' energy levels, I could actually control their energy levels by inducing their emotions. I learned how to identify when and how hard I could push an individual's emotions by the use of direct comments. I also learned how to throw out comments intended to get an emotional response, either good or bad, by mentioning things that would cause their energy levels to increase immediately for positively accepted information or decrease for negatively accepted information. Interviewing potential prospects and identifying what information led to positive and negative emotions was somewhat like playing the game twenty questions. Once I knew which emotions were truly driving these prospects, I learned how to tone my skills to a very high level.

Throughout my studies, I learned that during the closing process, if I started from the negative points and finished with the positive points, the prospects would finish on the points that they liked the best and the sale would take place. If I finished on a bad note, the sale would always fail.

Even though this ability not only to see the energy levels of these people, but to control these energy levels by manipulating their emotions was leading to me earning a tremendous amount of money from commissions, my true joy had nothing to do with the money at all. It was much more exciting to me to truly understand the people who were before me. I knew my personal abilities mixed with the accurate understanding of the sales profession could become an incredible amalgamation with triumphant results.

A sales career was always in the cards for me since childhood. When you are born with different abilities, you simply have certain paths opened for you to follow in life. Certain characteristics create doctors, while other characteristics create businessmen or astronauts or teachers. When you have a natural skill or characteristic and you try to do something else, for whatever reason, you almost always will fail because you're cutting against the grain. Sales was my calling in life, and I have always enjoyed the path and the people I have met while on my journey.

When I was eight years old, I used to buy gum and candy by bulk and sell the individual packs to the kids at school for a profit. I was the Wal-Mart of the playground, and kids used to line the sidewalks to see my offerings of the day. The school menu back then made my sales life very easy and profitable. Schools used to have a menu that changed ever so slightly from day to day, but never would you see a school menu change from week to week. I learned many years later that this was because school cafeterias never threw out food but kept all leftovers until they could be used again. Since all school foods of the 1970s were actually flavored preservatives and could last several years, the school officials felt keeping the leftovers for one week was harmless. As a side note, it should be pointed out here that there was an experiment that all of the kids were involved with on the playground. We took one of the school lunches out to the playground and hid it from the grown-ups' sight. The lunch was a pizza slice, a fruit cup, and a piece of something that was supposed to be cake. The lunch sat out on the playground for the entire year, and then on the last day of the school year, we took it out of its package and ate it. I swear it tasted better than if it had been new.

The food was so poor and tasteless schools wouldn't have to lock up the leftovers, because no one would ever try to steal any of it. They wouldn't even have to wrap it up in any secure, well-sealed area because bugs and mice were afraid of it and wouldn't go near it. I once saw a mouse accidentally get into a school lunch and then run straight to the Decon poison bait where it started eating the poison frantically to get the bad school lunch taste out of its mouth.

For me, this bland, tasteless daily offering created one of the greatest booms California had witnessed since the great gold rush days of the 1800s. Kids in my elementary school were bona-fide shoppers who would scour the playgrounds looking to invest their lunch money the best way they could. Due in part to my divine inspiration to fill a culinary need at the school, kids were offered many options of the day. Coming from intelligent families who reared them properly and instructed them to know the value of a dollar, these children researched the offerings for proper nutrition and taste. Okay, so they could care less about nutrition, but taste was an issue.

These kids had a choice: eat the school's daily helping of cheese "pizza," which was simply bread with tangy ketchup and bland cheese and a cup of lettuce or choose from a culinary array of Snickers, Mr. Goodbar, Red Vine Licorice, Milky Way bars, Three Musketeers, various gum flavors, and other sugary sensations. At the end of the day, the school meals continued. On "Taco Tuesday," they took the extra burgers from "Meaty Monday" and ground up the old patties to make the taco meat. Then they added the lettuce to say they served salads. The salads always made the parents happy. Wednesdays were always called, "Wacky Wednesday." I never understood why they called it that but they just did. Anyway, each Wednesday, they would either serve fish sticks or chicken sticks, and you could never tell which was which, with one exception; more kids died after eating the fish sticks. I guess it didn't preserve as well as the chicken. Because of the high risk of dying on fish stick day, all of the kids would bring a larger book bag to school that day in case one of their friends died as a result of lunch poisoning and they had to bring the kids' school junk home as a consequence. I lost four friends one year. The school always said their parents were transferred away, but we all knew no one ever really moved away. Thursdays and Fridays were much of the same, and for fear of losing some of the readers to wretched disgust, I won't go into any additional details of the school menu except to say a much belated, "Thank you," to the mindless souls who created the daily cuisine that started me on my way to fame and fortune.

My early mind, unlike the minds that created the school lunch menus, told me kids wanted choices around their meals, so I continued to expand my offerings. I even had to enlist a couple of chums to start handling the merchandise. I also quickly learned how to fire people when I found a couple of my buddies eating the profits. It was much easier to fire kids back then, because early on, I didn't have to involve the HR department and I didn't have to pay their unemployment benefits, although I felt obligated, so I kept paying their medical benefits for six months after letting them go.

It was during the early days of terminating these people that I also learned about jealousy and competition. The kids I gave the boot to decided they were mad that I was making money running my playground monopoly, so they opted to tattle on me. The cafeteria people, fearing that I was cutting in on their turf, were also mad at my flourishing business and decided they weren't selling enough of their goods either, so they also tattled. At first, nothing came from their tattling on me, partly because I was now supplying goods to the teachers, yard duties, and principal, so I kept on selling.

Things got a little rough for a spell, as I would find a cafeteria fork stuck in my bike tire at the bike rack. One day, when I opened my school locker, I found a "Wacky Wednesday" fish stick with a note attached reading, "Keep up your sales, and we'll make you eat a couple of these at one time!" I'll admit, the cafeteria ladies had me shook up with that note. I almost gave up my sales career right then and there. I thought about the situation at hand and decided that I simply loved sales too much to back down. Instead, for the first time in my life, I can remember thinking that it was okay to pay attention to my sensory capabilities and use my skills to their maximum potential. I wouldn't back down; instead, I would increase my volume and force the cafeteria people to go out of business. I thought to myself, *I'm eight. Don't fuck with me!* Then a nine-year-old walked by me and pushed me into my locker.

In all seriousness, this first sales process taught me some valuable lessons with respect to my visual differences. First, I learned to pay attention to what I was seeing when I offered someone a job, because even though this was grade school, what I had seen from my "friends'" energy levels told me all I needed to know about these people. I should not have hired some of them to help me, because it would only cause trouble for me later.

I also learned that you really can't create competition that will close down a school's cafeteria, once I got into trouble with the school and the cafeteria things started to spiral out of control. I also learned when a school gets pissed about a kid making extra income, the kid's parents also get pissed and make him show up to meetings with school officials. I also learned when a kid is in meetings with these school officials, it's not good to offer them a cut of the business even if their aura is telling you they want the offer. They'll keep a good cover in front of everyone else and yell at you.

I knew my parents were impressed, as I heard them talking to each other about me after the meeting. They were expressing their observations about how I was able to control the anger and other emotions of the people in the meeting very easily with my strategically timed comments and my direct responses. It was very interesting to me how I could control my surroundings and my audience with very little effort. I also knew by the very strong energy levels my parents were emitting they were extremely proud of the efforts and the sales results that their eight-year-old boy was achieving while at school, although they never admitted this while they were with the school officials. My father's energy levels and pride in me genuinely increased when the principal told him he had estimated that I was making a profit of roughly $100 daily from over one hundred children during the lunch hour alone, and the school needed the five hundred a week they were missing out on. Side note, I owned the best bike in school, and I paid every cent for it out of my profits. To protect my bike from the cafeteria ladies, I paid a couple of kids to stand guard, but the yard duties apparently have laws that supersede my paying them and the kids were forced to go back to their classrooms.

During this reformation discussion of what my activities would and would not include during school hours, I realized my parents never shared their enthusiasm with the school officials in spite of how they felt about my sales endeavors, which I could see clearly from their energy levels. It was then that I realized for the first time that everything is not and should not be discussed for the greater good of one's own self-interest.

As I got older, I was still selling whatever people were interested in buying, and in high school, many people were buying pot. I overheard a guy I knew at the time talking about a couple of marijuana plants that he had that were almost ready for harvest. He said he would be cutting the plants down and packaging the cuttings to sell.

I didn't care to smoke the pot, but I loved selling things, so I thought, *Why not pot?* I never felt bad about selling the pot or anything else because my philosophy has always been if someone is dumb enough to use drugs, then why not sell them what they want? After all, they will get the drugs they are after one way or another. I also have always held the opinion that there is no such thing as stealing when it involves an illegal substance. So when this opportunity presented itself, right or wrong, I had no issues taking the plants and selling the goods to people I knew would buy them.

I learned some hard lessons during my short career in the drug trade. First, the four brothers who grew the plants knew who I was since I went to school with them, and they were, without comparison, the biggest, meanest kids in school. The pot had been growing in an orchard across from the home where the brothers lived, and the day of the big pot plant heist, it had been raining fiercely all day, making the field extremely muddy. There was a large amount of clay in the dirt where I grew up, which would cake up and stick to the bottoms of your shoes when you walked through the mud. Luck had it that when I took the plants, all four brothers were home and saw me in the field pulling out their plants in the rain. They came charging after me. I knew they would have to run through quite a bit of mud before reaching me so I had some lead time to work with. I was able to get both plants out of the ground before they got to me and started running toward my brother and his waiting pickup truck across the street opposite the brothers' house. My brother had been instructed by me to wait with his truck running on the opposite side of the orchard. I didn't tell him what I was up to, just that I needed his help and I would only be gone for a minute. My brother was always as straight as an arrow, and he would never do a thing to hurt anyone, so he went along with everything without asking any questions. My brother quickly realized what I was up to as he saw me pulling the plants out of the ground in the field. He also knew how much trouble I was in, as he recognized who was now chasing me. En route to my brother's waiting getaway truck, with two very heavy, tree-sized marijuana plants under both arms, forty pounds of mud stuck to my shoes, and four angry giants chasing me while yelling a plethora of slang terms, I thought to myself, *Maybe this isn't a good line of retail goods for me to be selling.*

With that, I jumped into the back of my brother's truck and told him we should probably leave; he agreed, and we sped away.

Once home, I chopped the plants up into small pieces and stuffed everything into sandwich bags to sell my bounty more easily. This was when I first learned that pot smokers only smoke the buds and not the rest of the plant. Also, pot smokers take a special amount of pride analyzing the quality of the buds they are purchasing and really don't like buying chopped-up plants that resemble a bag of law clippings. I also learned when you steal dope, you should not take it from people who know you, especially if they are a lot bigger than you. I laugh at this as I think back to those days, because I can't believe I ever put myself in that situation.

When I was younger, I was able to hold my own in scrapes I got into, but these guys were big and they all hit hard. At the end of the day, I survived the beatings from the brothers and had reached my goal of selling all of the pot. Once I weighed the risks verses the rewards, I decided that it wasn't the business for me.

When I was in college, I sold solar systems door to door and was so successful I seriously thought about leaving college. I was making as much money as my father, who was an executive of a Fortune 100 company, and I got pretty cocky about how well my sales skills were developing. During this period, I honed my talents by listening to lectures from top sales-people who had come from many different walks of life. I bought all of the training tapes I could find, read all of the books, and went to all of the training classes I could find. I thought I had learned the secrets of selling, but my biggest lesson ever was right around the corner.

As I was breaking down my step-by-step sales process in order to train others to be successful, I had to think through each step. This was the first time in my life that I realized the potential powers my odd eyesight offered me. It was during this process that I understood I was able to see how prospects really felt about what I was saying. The aura surrounding people would shrink tightly to their skin if they were angry or upset. If they were happy or calm, their auras would increase in size. Understanding this, I started to refine my process even further by testing prospects' pressure points. In certain areas of the closing dialogue, I would push harder for the close than normal until I got the client to the point of anger where they finally told me to leave. I noticed during these points of the process, I could push them until the point where their aura was so thin that it almost didn't exist. I knew a thin aura meant anger and stress, and I had to be able to get people to this point to truly understand what they were worried about and then in the same meeting, knowing people only buy things when they have a comfort-driven thick aura, I would have to take the prospective to their comfort zone to get them to buy.

The success came to me after much trial and error, and once I understood which points of the sales process created the highest peaks of anger for the prospects and which created the highest levels of comfort, I softened my language on one side to create more comfort in the stressful areas and to get to my desired results of greater sales closing percentages. I learned to create penetrating language during the comfortable parts of the sales process. These changes ensured that clients understood why I was there and they were willing to give me the business as long as their goals were met by the service being sold and I was able to deliver the information to them correctly. As a result, I was able to eliminate all unnecessary closing pressures normally found in the sales process.

This is a little bit of reverse psychology; people are conditioned to resist sales closes, and they have a sense for where these will be presented. People are also conditioned to relax where no closing questions are usually found. When you ask closing questions during these nonthreatening periods, you generally get positive affirmations, and the sales process is much smoother.

As my skills increased, I learned of some special reading glass lenses that could eliminate blurring from one's vision. I was interested in these glasses, as I have always had blurred vision associated with my differences. I was able to track down a pair of these glasses and was shocked that they actually worked to eliminate 100 percent of any blurring when I wore them. To tune up my other senses that had been somewhat neglected over time because of my reliance on my extra visual abilities, I starting wearing these "magic glasses" all the time.

From the time I first started using the "magic glasses," I never took them off except for during sales meetings and more specifically during final sales meetings. By wearing the glasses during the initial meetings and discussions, I was forced to listen to what the people were saying, which allowed me to understand—really understand—their interests or lack thereof in my products or services. Once I had fully listened to everything, I would then remove my glasses, which would reveal the aura in its full glow to me so I could finish up the sale.

Thank God for the "magic" glasses!

CHAPTER 17

Late-Night Calls

The phone rang at 11:00 p.m., and the unfamiliar voice on the other end of the line said a man would call me in the morning. The caller would be interested in discussing recent tests performed on me at UCLA. I asked who the person was who would be calling me in the morning but was only told to take the call and not to worry about the identity of the caller. I told the unknown voice that I had no interest in talking with the caller in the morning if he couldn't tell me who the caller was or what the discussion was about. My phone rang as arranged by the voice from the evening before, but I did not answer. I assumed the interest in my UCLA tests would simply disappear. How wrong could I have been with my assumptions?

My job required me to fly roughly thirty thousand miles each month. It also required me to have periodic meetings with leaders of large national and international companies and with members of the Senate Finance Committee to discuss investment laws relating to corporate benefit programs and to give assurances these programs helped their constituents, the general economy, the plan participants and the companies that used these plans. When meeting with the congressional members, I had to fly into Washington DC's Regan Airport to attend meetings in the United States capital.

Assuming nothing more would come from the results found during my tests performed at UCLA, as I ignored the odd periodic calls requesting meetings with me, I thought life would go on in the normal, usual way. Others though were not content with my deliberate avoidance tactics, and my travel became both watched and controlled. Every time I went through an airport, I was met with a barrage of screening and delay tactics by the TSA. My bags were continuously checked to a level usually aimed at some-one on a possible terrorist list. My clothing was completely removed from my suitcase for each trip and often taken and returned at a later date. My magazines and paperwork were removed and examined; my shaving tools and toothbrush would be removed and returned to my hotel room later in the trip, each time with a TSA inspection tag attached. Because of this elevated level of inspection, travel became difficult. While all of this was going on, the secret calls increased in frequency. Finally, I clearly under-stood the effect of ignoring these calls, so I acquiesced to having a meeting.

When I finally took the call, someone recited a biography of my life from the time I was a little boy to the present. The caller's description of my life's historical events was fascinating, detailed, and unbelievably accurate. How could this caller possibly have this information with this level of detail? The details, many of them very personal, went well beyond the date of my visits to UCLA, and the information was much more revealing than anything that I had discussed with the university. It was the most amazing experience of my life. I realized quickly that there was no hiding from this any longer. Comments from the caller indicated that my unique visual abilities had been known about long before I had arrived at UCLA for my tests, and it was as though this secret caller's organization had expected that I would someday surface at a university to have my vision tested and authenticated. The secret caller said his firm simply waited for me to inquire about my visual differ-ences and come to my own conclusions before they became involved.

For the first time in my life, I truly understood just how different my vision was from others'. Growing up with these differences gave me many laughs, as I used my advantages to play games on others, play pranks on those around me, simplify dating situations, and help me close business by clearly reading the intent and emotions of the clients. I had been vary content with my abilities and used my visual difference to assure my happiness in life, love, and business. I remembered how easy it was to use my tools to make my first million dollars in business at a young age. I learned how to better navigate through life. I also learned how to keep quiet about my abilities, as I did not want people I worked with and lived with to feel threatened by my abilities. I also did not want to lose the advantage I had by divulging my secret. Only those individuals who were very, very close to me knew about my ability. This secret group had different ideas for me. They didn't care about the "kid games" I was capable of playing with my abilities; they were interested in much more important aspects of what these skills offered.

The time frame of this is very important to the urgency of the request for the use of my abilities. It was in the fall of 2001 when the secret calls started. America had recently been attacked in New York City, and for the first time in our history, we were faced with a new type of war called terrorism. Terrorism is a faceless fight where your enemy can be a neighbor, a spouse, a family member, or a coworker. Terrorism does not fight in the same manner as two armies lining up against one another in a clearly identifiable fashion. It offers the advantage to the attacker, not the defender. The attacker can come at you from many positions, and the defender has to defend against all unknown possibilities to ensure terrorists don't slip through a crack. I remember a comment I heard during a lunch with President George H. Bush: "Terrorists only have to be right once; we have to right 100 percent of the time."

President Bush's remarks shed light on the level of defensive strategies that are necessary to defend against terrorism. They also explained clearly why the government was so interested in obtaining any and all information around what was usually unseen.

The secret caller's intent was clear to me. I was being requested to view interviews with terrorism suspects to determine whether they were revealing all they knew or if they were lying during interrogations and identify if they had additional information they were withholding. In laymen's terms, I would be the equivalent to the US Customs Border Patrol drug-sniffing canines. These dogs sniff out what is unseen by humans. I would be using my visual abilities to identify what others could not see.

How would I accomplish this without giving away my identity and damaging my successful career? Don't get me wrong; I am much more interested in the welfare and safety of my country, but when you have a family, you do not want to jeopardize their safety and well-being either. This was the first time I ever realized the absolute scope and greatness of a compassionate government and understood the reach they had with the corporations that I relied on for my success.

For my family to continue on at the level of success that I had achieved in my occupation, the businesses that I worked with in the past and new customers just like them had to continue buying the products and plans that I sold or the Secret Service would have to find a way to compensate me at a significant income level. Otherwise, my family and I would suffer great financial harm, which could cause undue stress for my family and also cause my involvement to fail. Still to this day, I have no idea why sales became so easy, and like any good salesperson who suffers from an overactive ego, I would like to be able tell others just how awesome of a closer I really am. However, this just was not the case, as I had clients lining up to use my services and buy my wares. Having what I suspect were pre-informed and setup clients, I found it impossible *not* to sell my services, even if I tried. My income remained at record levels because of the ease of the sales made, and I had an incredible amount of free time to do other more important work.

Details of how life went on from here cannot be disclosed for many reasons, but it was never boring, as I met many corporate leaders and world leaders (some good and some bad); sometimes, I would be on US soil, and other times, I would be abroad in other countries. Sometimes these conversations would take place in public areas and sometimes within the confines of heavily guarded prisons. Many times, I would be directly introduced to these people, and other times, I would view them from a distance, but the reasons for my visual observations were always the same. I would evaluate them from an honesty perspective to determine if there was more they could offer or if there was something they were hiding.

I never tried to predict what the results would be from my observations, because I never had any complete data on the subject I was asked to evaluate. I only revealed what I was witnessing. The final evaluations were determined by those who had collected all of the data.

So here it was, in late 2001, after planes were allowed to resume flying in the US skies, I was about to walk on a plane heading to meet with congressional members to discuss business in Washington DC. In my arrogant view, these members of Congress only had one job: to meet with me. The real world is often very different than what's seen though one's own rose-colored lenses. They had a much greater responsibility: to protect our country against further attacks and identify these invisible enemies, some of whom lived amongst us in our country. My government rap sheet conveying my very private visual differences and capabilities popped out to some secret divisions like a firework display on the Fourth of July, and my world changed overnight.

My first trip through the newly increased airport security immediately proved to me that one way the military was going to start identifying potential terrorists was to round up people with my abilities in order to help properly sort out the bad guys from the good.

I have no problem with the government asking for my assistance, especially after what happened to the people in New York City; if the government would have called me, I would have said yes to help them without hesitation. It's never the intent of someone not to want to help; however, sometimes, when a poor approach is used by the asking party, the person being asked has no way of saying yes. The resulting sequence is like a game of cat and mouse. Combine that with my love of practical jokes and general dislike of people who abuse government power and personal information as a way to corner people to work for them, and you have the makings for a sequel to the movie, *Catch Me if You Can* in 3-D.

So there you go, the government secretly wanted me to work for them, but they didn't call me to ask me that; instead, they proceeded to use airport security to stop me in my travels. They had me go through the x-ray machines so many times that the radiation generated actually cleaned up a little cancerous skin problem I was having and I now have a slight glow to my skin when I walk outside in the evenings. Airport security would dump everything in my suitcases out and rummage around like a kid in a toy box looking for the illusive matchbox car. At the end of every flight, I would end up with a flyer saying TSA had gone through my bags and everything might not have been placed back the same way it was found. No kidding! If they had not left the flyer explaining TSA had visited my bag, I would have thought my bag had accidentally been placed in a gypsy camp where everyone had a chance to rummage through my things and purchase what they wanted, only to find out that I had no really nice things. They would become angry that my stuff was all crap and would start jumping up and down on my belongings and dragging them across their camp to display to everyone what horrible things I packed. Then they would reshuffle them into my bag for my enjoyment upon my arrival at the other end of my trip.

At first, I thought there had been a plane accident. It must have been terrible and people had to have been killed. I quickly realized that my somewhat fleeting imagination was once again running away with the show, because there obviously could not have been a wreck of the plane with which my bags traveled, because I was on the same plane. Just to make sure, I did the quick inventory that one would do to oneself after a horrible accident takes place: legs—check; arms—check; head—check; no puddles of blood—check; still alive—check.

Everything was okay with me, so why would someone assault my poor bag? What did it ever do to anyone? The first time your bag is assaulted, you say, "Eh, it's a random thing, and everyone gets their turn." But when you go through security eight to ten times a week and it happens on every flight, you begin to take notice. At this point, you can ask a faceless government entity such as the TSA to stop, and they won't; you can make a big ruckus, and they will harass you further; or you can shut up and take it and see what happens. With these great options, I shut up and took it... for a while.

Since I said nothing and since I had no idea why this was happening, it was very important to really pay attention to the contents of my bags. No matter what I put into the bags, I noticed things would be messed up upon arrival at my destination; yet nothing was ever missing. With this little bit of knowledge, I started placing items of some value in my luggage to see if these items would make it to their destinations, and they did. However—and this was where things got interesting—items that meant nothing, other than to cause a terrible inconvenience if they were removed, would go missing. On several trips, my underwear or socks or electric shaver would be gone. Sometimes, only one sock would show up and my toothbrush would go missing. The missing items would always arrive in a delivery package at my house prior to my arrival back home and never with a note or a return address.

Now, I truly love a good practical joke, and I don't care if the joke is on me or someone else, because it's the cleverness I appreciate. For a really good practical joke or prank to be successful, the perpetrator has to think through the entire strategy carefully, envisioning all potential pitfalls, and determine the best outcome. The best pranks sometimes have set-up periods that last months. The process that I was being put through was obviously one of a similar nature, and I was sure it wasn't intended as a prank. Knowing people the way I do, I was sure the personalities mirrored each other, because the processes used would have very similar characteristics. So the only thing I had to do was figure out why they were interested in my suitcase belongings and who the "they" was.

In the end, I knew if I was ever going to get control of my life again, I would have to take it back, so I said to myself, "Let the games begin."

CHAPTER 18

Living My Own Life

After walking off a plane in Vienna, Austria, with my family for a little business and a little R & R, I set my bag down only to see it immediately whisked away by someone unknown to me and thrown into a waiting car where it was then rushed away all within the first five minutes of our arrival. My wife, daughter, and I were speechless. I thought, *Here we go again. Why do they always have to come after my bags? If they have questions, why not just talk with me directly?* I thought about my poor suitcase being held against its will, tied down by ropes, its little roller wheels duct-taped so no one could hear the squeaking, all alone somewhere having its belongings removed from its inner cavities as it lay there helplessly. As a child, I never viewed the world through paranoid eyes, but when you are faced with these things happening to you so many times over the years, you really start to view the world differently. At first, you respond from a very confused place. As time goes on and these events continue to progress, you replace your confusion with anger and contempt because of the pain in the ass and inconveniences that come from the governments' paranoia.

As usual, I was entering a new country with no luggage, no clean clothes, no toothpaste, and no shaving kit, but well stocked with the hunger that engulfs you after you've been trapped in a plane for the last fourteen hours, so I decided the best solution would be for the family to find a nice place to get some dinner. I knew very well that once we got to the hotel, our luggage would be waiting for us as though nothing had ever happened.

You see, when you deal with the effects of paranoia over the years, you learn that even paranoid government agencies and their processes are very orderly and have normalized systems. I learned just to allow the government process to take its normal course of action instead of fighting it or even spending time trying to figure things out. In the beginning, I would go to the airline's missing luggage claim desks and let them know my luggage had not arrived. They would look into their computers to locate the missing bags only to find absolutely nothing listed. They could never find a relationship between my baggage claim tickets and any records in their computer locator system. Within minutes, TSA officials would arrive and escort me away from the ticket counter and assure me they had located my luggage and it would arrive at my hotel room shortly. They were correct; the luggage always did arrive as promised. The standard shipment process always included a hotel bellhop who had been tipped by someone to actually deliver my bags. The funny thing about my conversations with the TSA was they always assured me my luggage would arrive at the hotel, but I purposely always made it a point never to tell them where I was staying during my travels. Somehow, my bags always knew where to go. I just wanted to add this small note to give you a better understanding of the game playing that existed with this process.

Well, there we were in the inner circle of Vienna, which is unarguably one of the most beautiful cities in the world. If you have never visited Europe or if you have been to Europe but have never walked the streets of

Vienna, then you haven't lived. Vienna is one of the greatest cultural cities in the world. The city was under the royal leadership of the Hapsburg family, who firmly believed that symphonies, theatrical excellence, ornate architecture, and religious dynamics all played a part in creating cultural dominance. Vienna captures this dominance in its Inner Circle district where great parks and ornately beautiful buildings with their warm, glowing shops line the cobblestone streets. Bustling crowds converge on the warm, inviting symphony halls where concertos which had been written and performed years ago by immortals such as Beethoven, Mozart, and Haydn to outline operas and live performances, still transcend the world today.

Vienna is also one of the world's most renowned cultural dining centers; known primarily for its Germanic-influenced sausages and coffee, Vienna offers any cultural deviations that call to your taste buds.

With all that had happened since our arrival in the city, we tried to put the luggage issues out of our minds and settle in for a nice meal to get better adjusted to our new surroundings. During dinner, I started thinking about all of the times my sight differences had created havoc and disruptions in my family's lives, the pressures of years of multiple government harassment, and all the times my family had to fear or even worry about it when in the end nothing usually transpired. It was this constant annoyance of my family having to look over their shoulders that worried me the most, as I knew it was only a matter of time before they would grow tired and want to leave me and this ever-present fear. Who could blame them? This lifestyle was anything but normal, and the incidents that took place as soon as we entered Austria were just one more of the same on a long list.

Reflecting on all of the harassment my family had endured over the years and wanting it to stop, I couldn't get it out of my head how Vienna would make a great cover for me to trick the government into finally leaving me and my family alone once and for all. I started planning my disappearance without my family's knowledge so neither they nor any government intelligence groups would suspect that anything had happened.

I thought I could successfully pull off a disappearing act in Vienna for two reasons: First, knowing that I was on a family vacation, the governments would let their guard down on me. They would not suspect that a person on vacation would act any differently or take any risks that could involve his family's safety or security. Second, the city's beauty was mesmerizing and had a hypnotic effect on all individuals who came inside its walls regardless of how many times they visited. With these two advantages favoring my plans, I knew the best time to make a move and force a play would be during this trip.

My plan was simple: We would eat dinner on the terrace of the Hotel Bristol, a place where I had stayed many times—I knew the back halls and old stairwells would serve me well in my escape. I would wear a hat and a coat to dinner, knowing it was going to be a cool evening and also knowing my daughter never dressed warmly enough; I could give my daughter my hat and coat to keep her warm, thus creating a simple divergence. During dinner, I would tell my family that I would be stepping away for the evening to conduct a meeting after our meal together that would keep me out late. I also paid a lady a handsome tip to join the dinner table and escort my wife and daughter back to the room after we finished our meal. The plan worked marvelously, as my daughter appeared to a distant observer to be me, as she was now wearing my coat and hat, and the young lady who had my daughter's physique blended into the group giving the appearance that there were the same two women and one man at the table.

I had slipped out just prior to the time the young lady from the hotel arrived, so that the government workers who were casually tracking me would be none the wiser to what had just happened. I slipped into a back restroom where I had hid a change of clothing and some pieces of a disguise under the plastic lining of one of the waste cans. I quickly changed and took a position across the street from the restaurant where my family had been dining. My goal was to finally track and observe my trackers. My guess was that whoever was following me would show their hand once my family retired to the hotel. I also knew they would quickly learn I was no longer part of the trio once they realized that my daughter was in fact not me. This would be the challenge; how would they react?

How they ultimately reacted wasn't my real concern; I wanted to see who these people were once and for all, and I wanted to track them for a while to see where they retreated to and who they reported to. Tracking people who are supposed to be tracking you is very easy once you know who you are following, as long as they aren't eliminated from the operation completely after they lose you. The seriousness and importance of the operation often dictates the result of their losing you, or whether they are dismissed or kept on the case.

I knew my smart-ass escape game would really piss someone off, and it would not take long for my family to come under danger of a reprisal of the now angry team, who had just been tricked and embarrassed. When you deal with these types of issues for many years, you learn how to prepare yourself in unusual ways. My family and I always carried large sums of cash just in case we needed to disappear or lay low for several days. If you ever want to disappear, carry cash, because credit cards, ATMs, and traveler's checks always leave a trail to your whereabouts and you will be tracked down. Cash, on the other hand, is not traceable. How much cash you have determines how long you will be able to disappear for; the more you have, the longer you can stay hidden.

Even though I had not discussed my plan with my family before dinner, I had instructed them upon their return to the hotel room after dinner to leave the Hotel Bristol without their luggage and belongings and take the back stairs out of the hotel out into the alley. They were to keep walking through the streets past the great cathedral until they reached the opposite side of the city. Once there, they were to catch a cab and go to a bed-and-breakfast on the far side of the city where I had already reserved the room and paid in cash. The great thing about bed-and-breakfasts is they take cash and ask no questions. By having my wife and daughter do this, it would be almost impossible for them to be tracked. I knew my family's departure would have to be immediate, as there would only be a few minutes of time where my wife and daughter would not be watched once they figured out I had disappeared. I also knew that if we were going to pull this off properly and stop my family from ever being harassed again, one of three things would have to happen: I would have to disappear from my family forever; I would have to die; or I would have to create such a crazy diversion that no one would ever want to mess with me again.

Since I loved my family, I couldn't simply disappear. I'd gotten used to having my wife and daughter around, even though my daughter was a teenager and anyone who's either had or known a teenager knows the risk of having one around. People have always told me that I'm a wild person and a risk taker, and I used to believe them until I had a teenager in the house. Now I tell people I am nothing of a thrill seeker compared to those parents who raise multiple teenagers in their homes all at the same time, as those people understand what wild living is all about. I also knew I didn't want to die, not because I was afraid of dying but because of the pain you go though on the way to becoming dead. Once you're dead, what then? Lying around all day is not my idea of fun; plus, I don't like bugs, and the idea of bugs climbing around in my head eating all my dead stuff is not my idea of excitement. No, thanks. I'd die when I was good and ready, and it'd be a long time from then. Also, when I went, it would be the result of walking in front of a fast-moving train or truck so that I went fast and there wouldn't be any pieces left big enough for any dumb old bugs to chew on.

So a diversion it would be, but what could I do that would cause so much confusion and chaos for everyone to once and for all convince them to leave me and my family alone? Bingo! It would be the biggest prank and yet the easiest one I had ever pulled off. It would work.

Knowing I didn't have much time to work with, I immediately started individually calling all of the many secret intelligence agency contacts who had harassed me throughout the years in hopes that I would work directly for them. I told all of them that I was ready to talk with them and that I would meet them inside the Great Cathedral Vienna in seventy-two hours.

We would discuss the details and finalize our arrangements. I phoned all of the top international intelligence teams that had tracked me, tried to hire me, or tried to kill me over the years to set up a meeting, which I knew they would attend. I called the Australian Secret Intelligence Service (ASIS); India's Research and Analysis Wing (RAW); France's Directorate General for External Security (DGES); .Russia's Federal Security Bureau (FSB), which was the main successor agency of the Soviet-era Cheka, NKVD, and KGB; the Bundesnachrichtendienst (BND), the foreign intelligence agency of the German government; China's Ministry of State Security (MSS); the United Kingdom's MI-6—you have to call this group anytime you're involved with any covert operations, because if you don't, it would be like being a spy and never having watched any James Bond spy movies, as MI-6 is the spy unit that models itself after James Bond; Mossad, Israel's intelligence and covert operations group; Pakistan's Inter-Services Intelligence (ISI); and finally, the mother of all intelligence organizations, the CIA. The United States' CIA is the largest of the intelligence agencies and is responsible for gathering data from other countries that could impact US policy. As an American, you can always be proud of the CIA, because if they know others are bothering an American, rest assured you are protected to a much greater extent than any other citizen anywhere else in the world. There is no mistake as to why American soil is predominately avoided by bad people; the CIA doesn't mess up, unless you piss them off, then God help you.

I had all the intelligence organizations coming, so I decided I also needed to invite other contacts that I had met during my travels. I called my contacts at NATO to report that a top-secret world meeting would be taking place in Vienna's Cathedral Square in seventy-two hours and to have their people covertly meet there. NATO hates to be outmaneuvered by any of the intelligence groups, and when properly informed, they can be the most motivated people on the face of the earth; if there's an opportunity for some excitement, they are on their way. Since NATO ultimately informs the world's leaders of the international accords, I knew everyone important would soon be heading to my little meeting, which would be taking place in seventy-two hours in Vienna.

Knowing that the covert discussions would be elevated regarding this meeting and also knowing that everyone coming was much less informed than they usually were, I would have only one chance to get everything right, or I would in fact piss off all of the most powerful people in the world all at once, and I would most definitely be wiped off the face of the planet forever. So was I nervous? You bet your ass I was, and I only had a few hours to prepare.

Everyone was coming to the party, so now I just had to wait and pray that everything rolled out the way I hoped it would. Citizens around the world don't realize the magnitude of gatherings such as these. All countries these days keep teams scattered throughout the world so that they can have feet on the street immediately for situations as they erupt, and this was an eruption. Meetings like these created a fast and furious amount of intelligence buzz, or "chatter" as they liked to call it. The individual intelligence groups are very sophisticated and all operate on a premise of "stop at nothing" to get and manage the intelligence they are after, and this was what I hoped they would do and what I had to have happen if my plan was to be executed properly. When meetings like these take place, the parties generally like to prepare locations to ensure the safety of their people and the security of information. I didn't care for any of their teams' safety, and I didn't care about securing their information, so I set the meeting for seventy-two hours, knowing they would all have a very small amount of time to prepare, giving me an advantage. Also, with my family staying at an undisclosed location for the time being, I knew I could operate 100 percent effectively without worry that they would be harmed or at risk, so I was ready to play the game.

Remember, when I first called each of the different intelligence offices, I had told them I was ready to deal with them directly, but the "noise" going through their communications was obviously pointing out to them that many intelligence groups were converging on that same location at the same time. What they didn't know was why everyone was coming to Cathedral Square. Intelligence also picked up on the information that NATO members were en route and that world leaders had been informed of the international meeting. Intelligence leaders like to think their people never leak information and would never tell anyone anything to the contrary, but the reality is international news media from around the world had already communicated with their intelligence informants and were also en route to the same meeting.

The world's power was about to meet in Vienna, and I had no idea of what the outcome would end up being. What the f… was I thinking? I'm a quick thinker and have acquired quite a lot of street smarts through the years, but I have also learned that many quick, shoot-from-the-hip decisions leave you with very bad results. I just wanted to stop the harassment, so I decided to play a little prank on everyone who had been bugging me over the years, and now the whole world was about to get screwed, which led me to believe that maybe, just maybe, I had pushed the envelope a little too far. Just as I generally regretted pranking most people that I had pranked from the time I was a kid, I was now starting to regret this. Actually, it wasn't the prank that was about to take place, but the visions I had running through my mind of the ass whippings I was about to receive on a global level once these people realized that I had just played them for fools that started to concern me. The pranks I pulled when I was a kid were nothing compared to this one. Pranks like laying my sister's dolls around my brother while he was asleep and then taking photos and passing them out to his buddies or lighting dog crap bags on fire on a neighbor's porch, ringing the doorbell and running away leaving them to open the doors and stomp it out, or placing a couple of garbage cans in the middle of neighborhood streets and egging drivers as they got out of their cars to move the cans—these were all just fun and games compared to this monster of a prank. I thought to myself, *Oh well, I started this thing so now I have no choice but to finish it.*

In times of great duress, your mind quickly shops through all of the different scenarios and will generally point you to a great excuse or an exit strategy. This time though, my mind was saying one thing, "You're done, dude." My mind kept telling me I would soon disappear, and I would miss my family and soon become really, really dead. I didn't like what my mind was telling me, so I just thought about everything as quietly as possible.

I said to myself, *Think, Bob, think! What the hell can I do to fix this mess?*

"Holy crap!" I blurted out loud to myself. An idea rushed through my head as though I had a team of experts testing effective ideas from a so-phisticated think-tank. The idea was wonderful and should work; it would have to work, as I had no other options and my time was running out. All of the world's leaders would be there in a few short hours, and if I didn't craft an effective solution to this international meeting event, there would be some very embarrassed and pissed off people here, and I—or even worse, my family—would pay for this prank in blood.

My idea would not only work this time, but I thought it might be a permanent fix to the cat-and-mouse game that the world's governments had been playing with me over the years. Since I only had a few hours, I knew I had to work fast.

With its large tourist population, working in locations like Austria's St. Stephen's Cathedral is actually much easier than working on locations with smaller crowds, because it's easier to slip in and out unnoticed. Even if there are restricted areas, no one ever stops people from entering if the in-truders are confident and give the appearance they belong there. I learned this many years ago, and I used to bet my friends that I could get into any event or restricted areas and walk right past anyone guarding an entrance. The best highly trained guards in the world are very easily circumnavi-gated, because they are all trained to follow orders and never, I'll repeat *never*, make decisions for themselves. Knowing this gives a well-trained in-truder a decisive advantage when using the guards' own skills and training as a primary resource. Trained guards always look to cover their butts by having someone who outranks them give the orders. Every military base, big event or important function has someone who is ultimately in charge of everything. These head people never discuss things with low-ranking guards, which create a void of information between them and their own guards. The trick is to find the name of the main person in charge and call the guardhouse disguised as the leader. Simply pass on the alias that you intend to use when you visit. Once you arrive, the guards will not only let you in, but they will generally escort you to wherever you are hoping to go, because they think they are helping the main person out.

For superiorly trained guards, you may have to plan your actions steps a little better. One trick that has worked well over the years to distract skilled guards is taking on the role of a superior and conveying confidence in the conversation you engage in with those guards who need to be removed. Within minutes of your arrival, you have to have a very attractive female approach the guards while portraying a previously discussed leadership role. The guards will be attracted to the woman and will try to satisfy her desire to pass their post, but she will not have the proper authority to pass through. Even the best trained men guarding their posts are generally not trained well enough to counter these tricks, and most men are never trained to deal skillfully with pretty women in general. In their haste to help the woman, they will have forgotten about your presence, and you will soon simply walk on past them.

The toughest guards to get past are female guards and highly trained military security guards. Female guards do not fall for the easy trickery of sending a handsome man, unlike the male guards. When working with pretty women and highly trained and skilled guards, the perpetrator has to become either one of their superiors or invisible; I always find it easier to become invisible.

When I say I have the ability to become invisible, I need to explain thoroughly what I mean, how this works, and how practice can make anyone highly skilled in applying this particular art when necessary. The first time you try this and it works, you will be amazed. To fully understand how it works, you must understand the mind and how focused training actually plays into your hands and enables this to happen. Understand that when people are trained to spot things like people breaking in or guns or knives, they are trained very diligently to spot only those obvious things. They are trained so rigorously in the art of recognizing the concealed that they never even see anything if it is obvious; they are not trained to see obvious things, only unusual things, even if the obvious thing walks directly in front of them. Most of their training focuses on visual and auditory surveillance, and sometimes smell. If you are going to get past someone's sense of sight, you can't appear uncommon or unexpected in any way. Also, if you are going to get past someone's sense of smell, you must maintain a neutral scent at all times, never smelling like sweat, cologne, or perfume or anything else. If you are going to avoid being heard, you have to learn how to walk softly, hide your breathing sounds, and control your heart rate to the point where no audible sounds are coming from your body. These guards are so well trained that any noises or smell or recognizably trained occurrences will result in capture. If you are able to walk past a guard by taking on an unusual appearance and then they smell you or hear you in any way, your cover will be blown. This is where the term "blend into the crowd" comes from.

So if I was going to slip in and out of Austria's largest cathedral unnoticed to set up and complete my plan, I needed to blend in. Since the structure was undergoing remodeling, I decided my best strategy would be to impersonate a building inspector. By taking on the role of an inspector, I knew I would be given a personal tour of every square inch of the building, and my constant comings and goings at the building over the next couple of days would go completely unchallenged, leaving me to my own devices, which would be necessary in order for me to be able to set the stage and prepare for my visitors.

My plan was very simple. I would use my building inspector authority to rig cameras at all angles of the cathedral and wire these cameras to take constant video streams and send them to undisclosed Internet sites around the globe. These sites would be time sensitive, and if I didn't go into them with deactivation codes at ongoing intervals, the identities and contact information of everyone meeting at the cathedral would be made public to everyone in the world, thus rendering all of the world's intelligence teams, that had shown up at the cathedral, useless. If everyone agreed to leave me and my family alone once and for all, I would guarantee to keep everyone's secret identities intact.

Knowing that these people suffered greatly from paranoia and the fear that their identities might be leaked, I knew I had to somehow gather the group for a photo with all of them looking up all at the same time, but how was I going to accomplish that? Then it hit me as the great bells in St. Stephen's Cathedral rang out, "Bong, bong, bong," and everyone inside immediately looked up at the same time. I had my answer. The cathedral bells had rung every hour, every day, and every year at exactly the same time for almost a thousand years. It was obvious; I would have the photo stream coincide with the great bells. When they rang out, everyone would look up together and I would have my photos. These people wouldn't have any idea of what had just happened until it was too late to do anything to fix it.

There were twenty-three clocks in all at the cathedral. My plan was simple: keep all twenty-three ringing together precisely as they had done for the past several hundred years, and at the precise time of the scheduled meeting, set one of the clocks to ring one extra time. This extra ring would be vital for my plan's success because the clock's extra ring would have to be subtle enough to cause the spies' sub consciousness to force them to look up at the cathedral's bell hanging from the ceiling all at once so that the hidden Internet cameras' shots, which would coincide with the extra bell ring, could take full facial photos of all in attendance. These photos would transfer instantly to an Internet holding account that would have to have a proper code entered at different preset intervals during my lifetime or the spy's identities would be revealed for all to see.

To make sure they understood my message, I filled boxes with thousands of letters and tied them to the bell's gears; they would be pulled over by the gears at the time the solo bell rang for the extra time when all of the spies were in the cathedral. For safety reasons, at that time, I would be far away from the great cathedral sitting on a park bench with my laptop. I was close enough to the cathedral to hear her majestic bells trumpeting what I hoped would be an end to the years of running and hiding that my family had endured.

At the scheduled meeting time, the plan was set in motion. As soon as the bells completed their announcement, I was alerted to several e-mails that had arrived at my undisclosed websites, and when I opened the e-mails, I was pleasantly surprised at what I saw. Hundreds of secret intelligence team members all crowded into the great cathedral looking up to the ceilings as the bell rang out for a marvelous group photo and then thousands of copies of my notes were shown falling into their hands like confetti during a great parade. The expressionless looks on their faces said it all as they instantly knew what had just happened to them and they knew there was nothing any of them could ever do to me or my family again unless they wanted their secret identities revealed to the world.

We completed our Austrian travels without any disturbances and returned home unbothered. For the first time in many years, our luggage showed up properly and without incident, but there was a note in my bag, which read, "Thanks for all of the games we played over the years!"

www.ingramcontent.com/pod-product-compliance
Lightning Source LLC
Chambersburg PA
CBHW051125260626
47170CB00005B/1670